Gondwanaland

stories

by

Brenda Ray

Circaidy Gregory Press

Copyright information

Men in White Suits was first published in *The Derby Telegraph.*

Early Morning Rain was published in *Rogue Symphonies* (Earlyworks Press, 2007).

Gondwanaland was a winner in the 2011 HE Bates Short Story Competition and was published on the Northampton Writers' Group website.

ebook ISBN 978-1-906451-90-5
First published July 2013
paperback ISBN 978-1-90645189-9
First published June 2013

Printed in Hastings, UK
by Berforts Ltd

Published by Circaidy Gregory Press
Creative Media Centre,
45 Robertson St, Hastings,
Sussex TN34 1HL

www.circaidygregory.co.uk

About the Author

Brenda Ray has worked in librarianship, the theatre, and as a creative writing teacher. She is a mother and a grandmother, although she swears she doesn't look a day over thirty five. In the 1980s, she spent some years as a freelance playwright, with productions at Derby Playhouse and Croydon Warehouse, among other venues, and has a specific interest in silent movies. In the 1990s, she returned to education to take a degree in Photography and Film Studies at the University of Derby. She has now re-established herself as a short story writer, and cites her inspirations in this field as HE Bates, Dylan Thomas, Katherine Mansfield, Daphne du Maurier and JD Salinger. She has won a number of short story awards, and her book *The Siren of Salamanca* was published by Leaf Books in 2008.

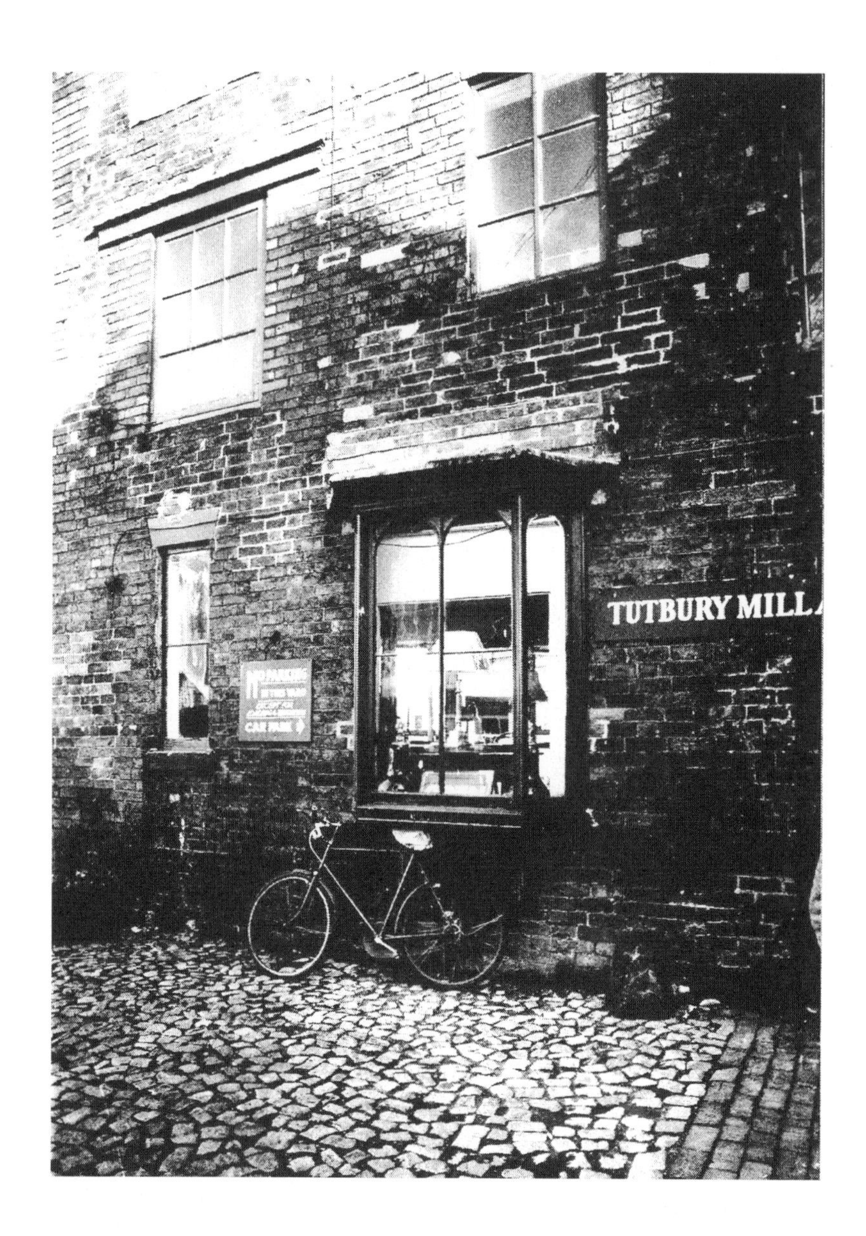
TUTBURY MILL
CAR PARK

Contents

Gondwanaland

Three things that don't exist:

a non-stick pan,
a non-iron shirt,
Gondwanaland.

Gondwanaland did exist. And it didn't. Well, it wasn't called that at the time. Because when it was there, there was no-one around to call it anything. And now it's gone.

Gondwanaland was a super-continent. It floated on an unknown sea when the earth was cooling. There was another super-continent called Pangaea, but that sounds like a patent cough medicine and doesn't have the same charm. But Gondwanaland... a name both ugly and beautiful. And above all, mysterious.

I go there sometimes.

There are no wars in Gondwanaland, because there are no people. Even if there were, there is no gold or oil or uranium to fight over because none of it has been formed yet. It's still solidifying, crystallising, percolating through the rock.

I poke at soggy Rice Krispies stuck in the plughole. Why do people have to have milk with them? Why can't they eat them crisp and dry like I do?

"Have you got your sandwiches?"

"Yes."

"Have you got your book bag?"

"Yes."

"Have you got that car you borrowed off Josh?"

"No."

"Well, where is it?"

"Dunno."

"Where did you last have it?"

"Dunno."

"Go and look for it, then. – Bike or scooter?"

"Bike."

I bundle the baby into her pram, swaddled like a tiny Russian grandmother. It's very cold outside. In fact, a heavy frost is twinkling on the pavement and rippling down from the trees. It may even be light snow. It is twenty past eight. By the time we get out of the house like some sort of small but stressed wagon train, the crispness underfoot is already melting and losing its pristine beauty. Gondwanaland has a mild and benign climate full of quivering greenery and doesn't have any litter.

"Can I have my sledge out after?"

"You haven't got a sledge."

"Well, if I had, could I have it out?"

"Ask Daddy."

What a cop-out. But it's easier. A bit of moaning continues, until he sees one of his friends. He hasn't got a sledge, either. Thank you, God. The two boys vanish ahead of me somewhere. Not sure why I still go to school with him, really. It's not as if there were any roads to cross. None the less, I worry. Where is he? Is he okay? When I reach the corner, of course, my son is waiting, small face aglow and gorgeous.

"Bye, then."

"Bye."

I shackle his bike inside the bike shed. Well, actually, I don't, since my hands are so cold I clip the lock together before I've wrapped the cable round the railing, and have to repeat the whole rigmarole all over, breaking several fingernails in the process. The baby is now beginning to squawk and I don't blame her. We have to go to our nearest supermarket to return a non-functioning kettle.

By the time we get there, Baby and I are both cold, especially as we have stopped several times to be admired (Baby, not me) which involves pulling back the hood so people can go "Ahhh." This is all very nice, but my feet are turning to lumps of ice. Baby has now nodded off, but not for long.

We wait patiently in the queue at Customer Services. Corals are forming in Gondwanaland. Limestone is being laid down very slowly.

"What can I do for you?"

"It's this kettle," I say, trying to sound polite but pained at the same time. "I've only had it eleven months and it's died on me."

"Oh dear."

"I need it for the baby's feeds," I add poignantly, hoping she won't remember me as the woman who came in a couple of weeks ago with a dodgy digibox. Electrical equipment takes one look at me and expires with its plug in the air.

She goes off to make enquiries. She's being helpful, but slow. So slow.

Baby has now started to squawk Big Time and the queue behind me has begun to shuffle. She comes back.

"It's very near to expiry date on this guarantee," she says.

"I know. I think they time things specially to clap out close to the date-line."

The queue is now sticking its fingers in its ears.

"She's hungry," I say, apologetically.

The Customers Services Lady says she can give me another kettle, but I'll have to have a refund on my card, take it to a till and start again.

I thank her. The queue sighs doggedly and moves forward. I smile at my shoes.

We chuck a few edibles, some orange juice and baby wipes in the trolley and wend our way, wailing, to the checkout. Before I reach it, a voice on the Tannoy calls out my name.

Panic. Oh my God, what's happened? My son's had an accident at school. The house is on fire…

I've left my card in the machine.

I give a Dame Hilda Bracket smile.

Card retrieved, we head once more for the checkout. Baby's given up and gone back to sleep. Lucky old her. By the time we get home, the washing I'd put out earlier has frozen on the line and the nappies and muslin squares now have the texture of anaemic Ryvita. Never mind, my son will love frozen underpants that stand up by themselves. A large bird circles overhead. It's making noises like a pig and I could swear it has claws on its wings and a beak like a bread-knife, but maybe I'm just tired.

I have to wake Baby up to feed her (typical) and eventually she nods off again, her downy little head against my shoulder. A couple of impressive burps ensue, then I put her in her cot and tuck her up. I lift my feet onto the settee and close my eyes. Eons slide away. A pale mist washes over everything, dissolves into a lavender sea, then there's a soft green shoreline, with gentle waves breaking on a silvery beach. Gondwanaland.

The Moon Shone Bright on Charlie Chaplin

I met a woman once whose father went to school with Charlie Chaplin. Not for long though, since due to the onset of their mother's mental illness, Charlie and his brother Sydney were bundled from one school or institution to another until Syd ran away to sea and Charlie joined the theatre. Funnily enough, I can't remember any more about the woman at all, except that I met her while I was giving a talk about silent movies in a village institute.

Afterwards, I was waiting outside for my taxi when I had an unsettling sense of apprehension. The following day I read that someone had murdered his wife a few doors away from where I'd been standing. Just an ordinary couple, it said in the papers, who kept themselves to themselves. Nobody ever thought anything like this could happen. But that's just by the way. What I'm actually saying is that meeting someone who knew someone who knew Chaplin was my own rather tenuous link with the great and famous.

Now, many years ago, my great grandmother ran away from home and became a pianist in a movie theatre. It wasn't what she intended, of course. Great grandmother wanted to be an actress. She was going to be a star. But as everyone knows, life isn't like that. Not for most of us, anyway. She left behind two children and a husband who loved her, and began a rampage of relationships that left broken hearts and babies all over the place, covered two continents, and ended in a workhouse in Gateshead.

So, after my talk, I stood out there in that cold and silent village street. And I wondered if my great grandmother had also stood in a dark village street, looking up at the sky, all those years ago, before abandoning her children and heading for the bright lights. She must have looked up too, and thought, there must be something else. There must be something out there, apart from babies and potatoes. But unlike Chaplin, she left behind a home of comfort and security and ultimately found only more babies and potatoes. And did she ever meet Chaplin? I don't suppose so.

I'd been telling the village women about Chapin's early days in poverty, about how those days in the workhouses and sordid tenements of Edwardian London had haunted him, and would later appear in the mean streets and cramped close-ups of his films, whereas my other hero, Buster Keaton, had spent his early years with his family of travelling entertainers in a covered wagon, crossing and re-crossing the great plains under a massive empty sky. And unlike Chaplin, all his pictures involved tiny, stick-like figures in a giant landscape. "Look at the films," I said, "and you'll see what I mean."

Rain dripped through the tin roof of the Institute, and I thought how those early shorts had been shown in places like this, accompanied by a single pianist who might just have been my great grandmother.

So when it came to question and answer time, this was how I met the woman whose father went to school with Charlie Chaplin. And then another woman came up to me, someone closer to my own age, and said, Hadn't I been on the Photography and Film course, years ago, when she'd been doing Librarianship on the next floor?

I said I had.

"I remember you," she said. She said her name was Aurelia Plum – a likely story, I thought. I didn't remember her at all.

"I used to know you," she said. There was a pause. "Didn't you used to go out with that Indian guy who was a political agitator at college?"

I thought for a moment.

"No," I said. "I actually went out with a guy who had a similar name to the political agitator, but it wasn't him at all."

"Oh," she said. "Are you sure?"

As if I hadn't known who I was going out with – even if it had been forty hm years ago. Actually, I'd rather not think about that. I smiled bravely.

"No," I said, "it definitely was someone completely different."

"Oh," she said, clearly deflated, her own tenuous brush with the great and famous diminished.

"Sorry about that," I said. Although why I was apologising, I can't imagine. And I didn't mention that a few years earlier, walking through London with the man I eventually married – who wasn't either of them, by the way – we'd passed a tall, vaguely familiar-looking man in a long overcoat and Nehru hat and all three of us had called out simultaneously,

"Hello, how are you? – Haven't seen you for ages!" and carried on our way.

And I said to my husband, "Who on earth was that?"

"Oh," he said, "it was –" and he mentioned the one-time political agitator, now a respectable broadcaster and correspondent for a national newspaper, frequently seen in a suit. And he'd never met him in his life before. So presumably, the ex-agitator must have thought, "Oh, wasn't that that girl people used to think I was going out with way back in the Sixties, who was actually going out with someone else?" And none of us were any the wiser.

"Yes, I do remember you," said my recently acquired acquaintance, Aurelia Plum. She stared at me intensely. "Didn't you used to be the tall blonde one with the glasses?"

"No," I said, "I was always the short dark one with the contact lenses."

And I went outside, where at least the rain had stopped. I looked up into the night sky, hanging over the windy wetness of the empty street, where unknown to me and apparently in complete silence, somebody was busy murdering his wife, and I thought how little any of us really know about one another. I thought about Chaplin, and I thought about my great grandmother, born the same year, for whom no fame and fortune ever came. No belated awards or chateaux in Switzerland for her. The woman I never knew, who fled her family and respectability, who sailed to America just before the *Titanic*, full of feckless dreams, returned disowned and penniless shortly before the *Lusitania*, and simply slipped into that long inevitable downward spiral until the doors of the workhouse closed silently behind her.

~ The End ~

Quite abruptly, it began to rain again, large gritty droplets plopping into my shoes. And I stood there in the dark, waiting for my cab.

The Hot Tub

I can't think what she needs that thing for. I mean, what person in their right mind would want to take a bath in their back garden? I can't imagine she took that many baths before she had it. Not from what I've noticed downwind, or from what I've seen hanging on her washing line. You could keep coal in that bra.

Now I've retired from work, I expect a bit of peace when I sit outside of an afternoon, but no sooner have I installed myself in my chair with a good book, then off it goes, *blurp, blurp, blurp*. And a cloud of steam billows over the begonias. The patio vibrates. "I'd just lie back and enjoy it, Mother, if I were you," my son remarked. I ignored him.

"It's a bit noisy, isn't it?" I said, when she first installed it.

"Oh, I'm sure you'll soon get used to it," she replied, in that patronising way of hers. Selfish cow, always has been. And he's no better. Pity he didn't spend his money repairing the fence instead of pampering her with that thing. Not that he's there often enough to notice. She'll have the milkman in there with her next.

I was sitting there the other day when a great big glob of hot water landed smack in the middle of my novel. Now, to make matters worse, she's started inviting her loud-mouthed friends and relations round. Edwin has gone off on another of his golfing holidays, so mega-mouth sister is also marinating in the cauldron every afternoon, bubble, bubble, toil and trouble, blurp, blurp, shriek, shriek. Then in the evenings, here we go again, *bubble, bubble, blurp, blurp, shriek, squawk, splat* as another fat, damp bum hits the decking. And they're drinking, as well. *Shriek, squawk, cackle, crash*, another bottle hits the bin. Party time at the Boozy Jacuzzi. Something must be done. Nothing too obvious. Nothing illegal.

I head for the craft shop. Green mixed with cow-dung brown, perhaps…? "Does it stain skin?" I enquire, brandishing a mammoth-sized packet of dye.

"Not if you follow the instructions," they say, helpfully.

I wait until dark before taking advantage of the gap in the fence. The dye should spread out nicely as the water heats up. She tends to turn on the Jacuzzi early in the afternoon. I start off with green, the powdered variety, so it'll colour slowly by degrees.

Sure enough, next afternoon, here we go, *blurp, blurp, shriek, squawk.* I lie back in my recliner and bide my time. As it gets round to feeding time, I hear them squelching and splatting across the decking.

"That's funny," I hear someone say.

"What?"

"My legs look green."

"Trick of the light," I hear Caroline reply. "It's just the reflection from the trees."

They go indoors. Tomorrow is Sunday. After breakfast, I note towels on the washing line. Yes, they are definitely tinted. And a rather sickly bikini.

"Hey, Caro –" it's Mega-mouth – "your tub's looking a funny colour!"

Just you wait.

"It'll be alright when the water gets hot."

Indeed it will. Green and brown with a shot of purple curdling round will be lovely. The purple is a liquid dye, so it should produce a particularly interesting effect.

By mid afternoon, a great deal of shrieking and squawking is going on, then I hear the hot tub clonking and gurgling into action.

"Oh my God!" (Mega-mouth again.)

"Now what?"

"Come and have a look at your tub!"

Shriek, squawk, gurgle, hiss. I hear switches being applied. More steam rises above the begonias. Bad language ensues. Tut tut. Shocking.

Then I hear Caroline bawling into her mobile. She's phoning *Severn Trent.*

"What d'you mean, you can't come till Tuesday? My water is contaminated!"

Sniggering silently, I go inside. On Monday, I go to the health store and buy a packet of tapioca.

Tuesday. Nobody appears all morning, though, thank goodness, Mega-mouth has gone home. By four o'clock the *Severn Trent* van pulls up outside and a bloke in white overalls emerges. I hear Caroline berating him loudly for being late. Evidently she hasn't looked at the tub for some time, and by now nasty whitish globules are floating in it. After much discussion and frustrated bellowing from Caroline, I can see *Severn Trent* Man between the slats in the fence scooping something into a jar.

"Frogspawn? It can't be frogspawn!" bawls Caroline, as *Severn Trent* Man disappears down the path holding his jam jar aloft.

Next morning, a van labelled *Pools4Yu* pulls up on the drive, and I have the pleasure of hearing the hot tub being drained with a satisfying gurgle and slurp.

Thereafter, several days of peace. *Severn Trent* Man and *Pools4Yu* Man make numerous forays and depart with much shaking of heads. I pass Caroline on the path. "Problems with your water?" I enquire solicitously.

"It's that effing hot tub," she snarls. "It's not the tub and it's not the water, so what the hell *is* it, might I ask?"

"Oh dear, Caroline, I *am* sorry. And it must have been *so* expensive..."

She snorts and bangs the front door. Next day, alas, the tub is up and blurping again, pure and sweet, presumably. Steam billows out across the begonias and the patio is shaking like a cakewalk. Something must be done.

It's then I remember the fisherman's maggot shop. *Tommo's Tackle.* Very tasteful.

"Give me five boxes of your very best," I say to the man behind the counter, possibly Tommo, but who cares? He sports pebble glasses and a greasy mullet.

He looks slightly agog.

"It's for my husband," I smile. "For his club. What's the sell-by date?" I enquire, as he plonks several plastic boxes of wriggling obscenities on the counter. I try not to look. "I mean, how long can you keep them before they hatch?"

He tells me. I thank him and depart with a carrier bag at arm's length. Later, I pack my suitcase.

"Ooh, you don't know what you've missed," says my other-side neighbour, a couple of weeks later. "We've had *Severn Trent*, the public health inspectors, flies everywhere, we've even had people from the press…"

"Oh *lord*," I say. "How *awful*."

"All started from that rotten hot tub of hers, they reckon."

"Oh *dear,*" I say. "I obviously picked a good time to go on holiday, didn't I?"

Later, I commiserate with Caroline. She looks haggard and smells of drink. I am almost on the point of feeling sorry for her.

"I expect you'll be getting rid of that wretched Jacuzzi, then?" I say, sympathetically.

"No, it's all been sorted. Some sort of fluke of nature," she says. "The public health inspector said it was quite unprecedented. He'd never come across anything like it before. But they've shifted all the maggots, the tub's been totally disinfected and everything's been given a clean bill of health."

Arse. Bum. Tit. Just my luck.

"That'll be a relief," I say.

"Yes, and I can start using it again today."

Bloody hell.

"Weird," I say. "Like those plagues of frogs that fall from the sky. Or locusts, like in the Bible. Could it have been, do you think?"

"I've no idea," she snaps. "But it's sorted now. Thank God."

I smile benignly. "And then there's global warming, of course. That's what comes of messing about with nature. Remember those stories about people buying pet turtles and flushing them down the toilet? Makes you think, doesn't it? You never know what might be down there…"

"Oh don't!" she moans. "I need a drink!" As I go in to unpack, I hear another bottle hit the bin. Then later, I hear the bloody tub start up again.

After I've hung my washing on the line, I sit and mentally take stock of things. Edwin is due back tomorrow, I gather, and is bound to notice the amount of bottles in the bin. Golf, not booze, is Edwin's vice. Maybe I'm still being too subtle. *My* husband (RIP) would have taken a more direct approach. In fact, he'd probably have chucked a couple of piranhas…

Suddenly, I have an idea.

Mr Mu and Mr Qo have been running the jokes shop for longer than I can remember. *TRICKS AND JOKES. ORIENTAL NOVELTIES* it proclaims over the door. It's the only place in town where you can get carnival masks, paper fans, greasepaint, sea monkeys and clockwork teeth. You can buy stink bombs, itching powder and even less desirable items, stacked neatly on the shelves with labels like *Naughtee Doggee* and *Fartalot.* Mr Mu and Mr Qo also act as agents for slightly dodgy entertainers whose dog-eared notices are taped to their door. I had to complain about the escapologist they'd recommended for the fête. The fire brigade were not amused. However, they seem to have forgotten that, and greet me like an old friend. Mr Mu and Mr Qo don't say much, but they giggle a lot. I suspect they take enormous pleasure in their work.

I explain carefully what I need. "It's for my grandson," I say. "To frighten his friends with." They nod earnestly.

"Remote control, very lifelike. Scare pants off anybody," they assure me. "Rechargeable batteries." Grin. Giggle.

I thank them profusely and depart with a long parcel and a smirk. On the way home, I invest in another packet of dye.

Edwin has returned. I note his golf trolley by the garage door. Later when I sit outside, I hear raised voices. He is whingeing about her drinking. She is whingeing about the problems she's had with the hot tub and how much the neighbours have been complaining. He is whingeing about how much it cost.

"Well, I'm telling you, Caroline, if there's one more problem with that thing, it's going. Any more complaints or infestations, and it's going straight to the tip. Do you understand?"

"Well, I'm not going to stop using it just to please you – *or* the poxy neighbours!"

Tut tut.

"Caroline –"

I hear a muffled oath and the sound of a door slamming shut.

Now the nights are beginning to draw in a bit, I've noticed Caroline has started using the tub a little later. Perhaps she feels the darkness is more romantic. Or maybe she just thinks Edwin won't notice how fat she's getting.

Edwin has stormed off to unpack. Caroline has lit a fag and is probably opening a bottle of something. I can smell the smoke through the open window, and yes, there goes a cork. The woman's a slut, let's face it. She'll drink first, then come outside. She won't get into the tub till she's finished her cigarette.

I creep silently to the gap in the fence. We who are about to *dye* salute you, I mutter, sprinkling *Aubergine Ardour* into the water. (Eat your heart out, Noel Coward.) Then follows my little amphibian friend.

"See you later, alligator," I murmur, as he glides away. And I sit back with the remote control wand and wait.

Caroline's screams are positively bloodcurdling. Almost the *entire* street turns out. There follows a good deal of ooohing, tutting and head-shaking. Caroline is pissed. Edwin is livid. I am smug.

Caroline is eventually led off whimpering to bed. While the kerfuffle is going on, I retrieve my amphibian friend from the tub and shove him hastily under an old blanket in the shed. I really must ask Edwin nicely to repair that broken fence panel.

As I sit on my patio the following afternoon, Caroline is conspicuous only by her absence. I lean back contently in my recliner. I pick up my book. Once the sound of pickaxe-wielding and of bottles being chucked into the bin has died away, the only noise to disturb my peace is the rumbling of the concrete mixer.

The Cliff Walk

From where he stood, the path wound away from him, looping down the shallow cliff in lazy zigzags. The land sloped below in planted terraces, now dead and colourless in the winter haze. A few plants remained, thrift, sea lavender, dried tufty things, and a few unpruned roses, now just shrivelled buds and half-open flowers, fossilised, turned into stone. Beyond them, a drift of ornamental grass, bleached and feathery, shielded the rest of the slope from view. The land was restless, waiting for the spring. Only the sea was implacable, lapping the shore below with an almost imperceptible hiss just beyond his range of vision. To his left the headland rose sharply, the path eroded and close to the edge. To his right a few diffident ripples touched the inner curve of the bay with a tiny silvery line, soft as the dabbing paw of a kitten.

As he made his way into the shelter with his newspaper, relishing the calm, he noticed a figure on the lower zigzag of the path, much closer to the sea, which at the moment was almost indistinguishable from the sky. A woman was standing by the railing, silhouetted in charcoal grey against a pearly backdrop of sea and sky.

He sat inside the shelter, opening his newspaper, glancing at the columns, picking out items at random but with little interest. The hotel's Full English Breakfast lay across his stomach like an oil-slick and he fished in his pocket for a tablet to quell it. He'd have to reduce the cholesterol. He glanced at the Stock Market Page, sighed, turned it, looked away. He needed to forget all that stuff. The woman was still standing on the loop of the path, looking out to sea. He studied the sports pages with equal indifference. Looked up again. She was still there. Hadn't he spotted her there last evening, after he'd put his bags in the lobby? Hadn't she been walking up and down the path even then? Something about her struck him as unusual. But really, he had only noticed her because there was no-one else to see. She was aloof, oblivious, alone. A figure in a landscape. An old photograph. A movie still.

He rolled the paper under his arm and walked out of the shelter and along the top promenade, past the locked kiosks and shuttered amusement arcade towards the town. As he turned away from the sea, he looked back for a moment and saw the woman also walking, away from him along the cliff walk, down towards the unseen shore.

Later, in the pub, old photos on the wall showed how little the town had changed. Only the fretted shore to the far right of the bay had altered, the cliff eroded and slumped in boulders onto the beach, while the left of the bay, protected from the tides, had scarcely changed at all. By the inlet though, close to where he'd been standing, a chunk of cliff must have sheered away. Along the front, in Edwardian times, the hotels and narrow boarding houses looked much as they did now. Only the cliff walk seemed different, for where there'd been formal planting along the paths, and wooden benches, it was now more random with drifts of sea-grass around the white, curved Art-Deco shelters, still gleaming like freshly peeled haricot beans. Across the water, another tribute to the 1930s, a white, gleaming, modernist hotel, its sinuous lines pasted into the curve of the bay. The same scene in a framed monochrome print, showed, lurking on the horizon, the gaunt black profile of a destroyer. When he walked out again into the chill of a winter sun that had finally emerged from the mist, a thin wind had whipped up the sea, and the woman on the path had gone.

Later that evening, sitting in the hotel bar, he thought about the woman on the path. Something about her. Something that didn't fit. Something elusive, as though she was both there and not there. He thought about the photographs in the pub. The Art Deco shelters and the '30s hotel. They'd have seemed modern then, chic, streamlined, different from the rest. Like the woman on the path. Elegant. Different.

It was the clothes, he thought. Something about the clothes. But he could not bring them to mind. Clothes were not his thing. The '30s, maybe the '40s. The War, he thought. Things would have looked different then. Barbed wire and minefields. Troops in the hotels. Blackouts at the windows. The south coast would have been the front line.

"What was it like here in the War, do you know?" he asked the barman. He looked puzzled. The barmaid smiled and shrugged. They were Polish and did not understand.

Later, up in his room, he opened the curtains a few inches and peered out. For a moment, he thought he saw the woman walking along the upper level of the prom, and then she was gone.

The next morning, the mist was back. He neglected to buy a paper, and walked along the same route as the day before, but now the sun was breaking through and the ground and the grass and the railings glittered softly with tiny pinpricks of dew. As he reached the shelter, he looked across towards the still-invisible sea, and there she was, the woman from yesterday, leaning against the railing lower down the path. It was the clothes. Definitely the clothes. She wore a coat that was short, belted at the waist, the shoulders wide, and she carried a handbag shaped like a box. Her heels were high – not stilettos, but chunkier and the soles were thick, making her look taller and slimmer, perhaps, than she really was. Platforms, that was what they were. And she wore a hat, trilby style, pushed over on one side, thick long hair brushing her shoulders. He knew, even though he could see only a silhouette against the backdrop of mist, that the face under the hat was beautiful, that the mouth was bowed and full, the lipstick scarlet. As he watched, she moved away from the railing and started to walk, slowly, first one way, then the other, watching, waiting, her unseen eyes fixed upon the unseen sea. As he watched, the sun broke through, still low and wintry, casting around the figure of the woman a curious halo that clung to the edges of her body and the railing beyond in a fuzz of primrose light.

"Nice to see the sun, dear," said a voice close behind him. He turned and saw a woman sitting inside the shelter.

"Sorry," he said, for he must have jumped. "Didn't see you there."

"I said, nice to see the sun."

"Yes. It's been a long winter. We need a bit of sun. – Quiet, isn't it? Still, that's what I came here for."

The woman smiled. She was old, very old.

"Quiet," she said. "Quiet as the grave."

"I can't argue with that," he said.

"What you doing here then, dear? Hardly holiday weather, is it?"

"Oh, just a stress-busting break," he answered. "You're local, I suppose?"

"Londoner, originally," she said. "Been here a long time now, though."

"I'm curious, he said, "that woman over there – do you know her?"

"Oh, she's just a poor, sad creature, dear."

"You know her, then?"

"Of course I do." The old lady smiled again. "Just waiting for her young man, that's all." Her voice was comforting. The slight London accent, old-fashioned, amiable. An Ealing Studios kind of voice.

"– I thought for a moment…" He almost laughed. "I must be going barmy."

The old woman waited.

"You know her, then?" he asked, reassured.

"Oh, I know her very well."

"I'd like to meet her," he said. "She looks so elegant. Different."

"Yes, they don't dress like that any more, dear. In those days, we always did our best, you know, even though times were hard. To look nice, you see. Kept our spirits up. None of those awful track suits then. None of those horrible jogging bottoms. And those trainer things – what are they training *for* exactly? Most of them are too fat to walk to the end of the road."

"She's like someone in an old movie," he said. "The sort they used to show on TV on wet Saturday afternoons."

"Yes, dear, I know what you mean." The old woman smiled. "We were real women then."

"So you were a glamour girl too, were you?"

There was a pause. She smiled again.

"Of course," she said. "We liked to keep them interested. But then, in those days, you never knew if your man was coming back. And if he didn't, whether he'd been killed or just found someone else. You never knew."

"No, I suppose not."

"Can't trust 'em, dear. Men. – You married, dear?"

"Divorced," he said.

"Sad."

"Amicably enough," he added.

"They all say that, dear. No, you can't trust 'em. Can't stand 'em, myself, men. Still, I shouldn't say that to you, dear, should I?"

"No, you shouldn't," he said, half-smiling.

"Callous bastards, men," she said. "I know what I'd do to every unfaithful bastard, I'd get a knife and gut them like a kipper, that's what I'd do."

"Bloodthirsty," he said, still half-smiling, but with a little less confidence than before.

"Maybe, dear," she said. "Or maybe not."

The other woman, the woman on the path, had stopped pacing now and stood still in her halo of primrose light. Then she started to move, slowly, towards them. Although her face was still hidden, he knew suddenly that it was not beautiful, that her lips were not full and red, that she had no lips at all.

Suddenly the haze of light surrounding her went out, and the sea was the colour of lead. It was bitterly cold.

"The woman," he said, and a chill of another kind gripped his heart. "She's gone!"

"Trick of the light, dear, she's coming this way."

"Then, where – ?"

"She's coming, dear, can't you see her? If she'd gone the other way, she'd be over the edge. It's closer than you think. The light's funny here, you know. Reflections off the sea and the white cliffs. That's why people go over the edge, they say. They lose their bearings. She's so close, you could almost touch her."

He knew it was too late now to say any more. Strips of mist were blowing across the cliff walk, surrounding them, enveloping them in nothingness.

"The young man," he said then, because there was nothing else left to say, "Did he ever come back?"

"No, dear," she said. "I'm still waiting."

A Shoe in Priory Park

It was almost silent in the park, apart from a faint cooing from the wood pigeons, and even they seemed dispirited. A few leaves, left over from the autumn, still drifted from the lank trees and into the lake, where they floated like small dead fish before settling into the mud. The sky was dove-grey, streaked with the occasional faint slash of hazy sunlight but over towards the house itself, it was becoming darker. Occasionally, a crow or possibly a rook would utter a few distant clacks and then stop again. We shouldn't have been there, of course.

"I think it's going to rain," said Imogen. Imogen was my cousin. She was four years older than me, and nothing seemed to bother her much. "I expect we'll get soaked." The sky was now the colour of dirty pewter and a few heavy spots fell loudly onto the surface of the lake.

"We could go in the house," I said. My mother would *not* be pleased if I came home soaked to the skin again. Not to mention plastered with mud. These things seemed to happen when I went out with Imogen. It was okay for her. Her father was always out at work and her mother was heaven knows where.

"It's horrible in there," said Imogen. Adding after a moment, "I like it, though."

We trudged up the slope towards the remains of the house. It still had most of the roof on, but bits of it were missing, and the doors and windows gaped. Priory Park, you see, was not a public park as such, but an old estate that had been given over to the Council a few years before the War and nobody knew what to do with it. Eventually, war broke out and the troops took over. Nissen huts were put up on one side of the park and a concrete parade ground constructed, bits were wired off for target practice, mysterious things went on in out-buildings and the troops trashed the house, which was why it was in the state it was today. It was, in other words, a paradise for naughty children with nothing better to do.

Imogen and I preferred the far side of the park. Not the bit where the parade ground had been and a few displaced families were now billeted in the remaining Nissen huts. We'd been chased away a number of times by angry women with brooms, or cat-called by wild and wary children. We liked the bit of the park that sloped down towards the lake, where hardly anyone ever went. The lake was now overgrown, and only a few torpid fish were spotted between the weeds. Probably the rest had long since been caught and fried by passing soldiery, whose discarded cartridge cases and dented mess tins could still sometimes be found amongst the straggly grass. There were a few KEEP OUT signs here and there, especially near the woods, which were reputed to hide unexploded ammunition, but Imogen said that didn't really matter. Imogen was pretty well bomb-proof, as ten year-old girls go, and loved to scare me telling how a bomb had once gone off and blown their garden wall to bits while she was standing a few yards away on the lawn. Bits of wall and soil went right over their roof, she said.

The War, to me, was something that had always been there, something far away. The War was a shadow, a distant memory, a name. The War affected the food we ate, the clothes we wore and the things we did that were routine, and our parents didn't want to talk about it. And now it had gone.

Imogen's dad, who was my Uncle Brad, had not returned straight after the War, but had been in something called the Army of Occupation. Imogen's mother, however, was a different matter entirely. Imogen's mother came and went. Mainly, she went. Imogen's mother's name was Melita. She was never known as Aunt or Auntie, not to me, anyway. Melita was simply referred to as "Melita", with a sort of cool distaste. Melita's name, in our family, at least, was mud. Like "The War", "Melita" was mostly just a name, for I rarely saw her. "Melita" held a sort of hidden glamour, an evil yet attractive allure, a seductive *something* that was hard to explain, though anyone remembering a child's sense of curiosity will know exactly what I mean. Melita was an unusual name, highly memorable. – *After a grand-daughter of Queen Victoria*, Imogen said, grandly, *and I'm named for somebody out of Shakespeare.* Melita, according to Imogen, was "doing war-work" – what kind of war-work was never explained. Or she had to go into hospital. Or she was having a holiday. Or something. In fact, just about everything about Melita was a bit of a mystery. She was an orphan. She was brought up by nuns. When she was about sixteen or so, wisely, or perhaps on reflection, not, she departed the convent and embarked on a life more interesting. And that was about all we knew about her.

Once Uncle Brad returned on a permanent basis, Melita disappeared entirely, leaving only a wardrobe full of clothes that presumably she didn't like much. There was also a vanity set, an old orange Tangee lipstick, a pair of pearl earrings, some rings on a stand and a bottle of *Evening in Paris* on the dressing table. My mother also had a bottle of *Evening in Paris* which someone had given her, entirely unused, and when I asked her why, she said it was the sort of cheap perfume that Melita had used. Then she checked herself and said she simply didn't like it. I didn't like it much either, having tried it a few times when my mother wasn't looking, and then filled the bottle with water so it went all milky, but nobody noticed. It was in a pretty bottle though, deep blue, in a sort of spiky tower shape, and whenever I saw it, or smelled it on anyone, I always thought of Melita.

Of course, Melita *hadn't* disappeared entirely, but was seen on odd occasions by my parents or the inevitable gossipy neighbour, flitting in and out of shops or cafes in various parts of town, dressed up to the nines (or tarted up, as the less kindly would put it) often in the company of a man, though not necessarily the same one. This was not unusual for Melita, who had the ability to vanish like smoke if the need arose. I knew that Imogen tried on her clothes and jewellery, not to mention the infamous Tangee lipstick, when Uncle Brad was out. However, she rarely mentioned Melita. Once when I was brave enough to do so, the response was simply, "Oh, she's gone on a holiday", which I knew in my innermost mind wasn't true. However, to avoid embarrassing Imogen, I never asked again.

The rain had begun in earnest, a thick persistent drizzle that looked as though it might rapidly turn into the proverbial stair-rods, so Imogen and I quickened our pace as we scrambled up the slippery slope towards the house. It was now entirely silent apart from the increasing rattle of the rain. The rooks or crows had finally shut up and there seemed to be no-one else around. We scurried inside a gaping doorway and shook ourselves like small wet dogs.

"Phew!" said Imogen.

We stood just inside the door, to catch our breath, before peering into the gloom within. As our eyes adjusted to the dark, we slowly became aware that we were not alone after all. We stood there, dripping, listening. From one of the adjoining rooms, a slight rustling came, followed by faint moaning and gasping. Imogen pointed to her mouth, then gestured silently, *Follow me.* Holding our breath, we tiptoed softly in search of the sounds.

The inner doors had long since been removed from their hinges, so we were able to peer inside the room without any difficulty. There was just enough light filtering through the dirty window to see what appeared to be a heap of animated clothing on the floor from which emerged a woman's leg, and I heard Imogen gasp, then the bundles of clothes separated and Imogen gasped again. A bulky shape detached itself from the woman on the floor, and bawled in a thick male voice, "What the hell are you doing in here? Get out!"

Imogen and I leapt away from the doorway as the man rushed towards us.

"Don't you know you're bloody trespassing?"

We cowered in an alcove as he rushed past us. Then he stopped, realising we were still in the building. He turned and bawled something incoherent as the second figure in a state of disarray rushed out of the room, holding its shoes in its hand. The shoes were red and black, with platform soles. I heard Imogen give another gasp, then we dived past the man and out into the rain.

The man bellowed at us as we made a dash for the bushes, "Get out! And if you ever tell anyone you've seen me, I'll bloody kill you! – And that goes for you, too!" – he yelled as the woman rushed past us and disappeared into the overgrown shrubbery. I only caught a glimpse of her, but her long wavy auburn hair, so like Imogen's, was more than enough. The woman was Melita.

We didn't stop to see where she went. Or even turn round to see if the man was following us. We just kept on going until we came to a hole in the hedge and left Priory Park behind. Typically, we'd come out on the wrong side of the park, and it took us forever to get home. Neither of us spoke, and when we separated Imogen was still as white as a sheet. She went home to her empty house, and I carried on towards home, soaking wet and covered with mud, to be told off by my mother.

By the time my mother's exasperation had worn off, I decided it was not a good idea to say where we'd been or what we'd seen, and the whole incident would have been swept under the carpet if a few months later, Melita hadn't disappeared. This time, as it turned out, for good.

Melita, as we later learned from the press, had been living in a rented flat, where it seemed she occasionally entertained male visitors. Her landlady, noticing she hadn't been around lately and letters were piling up for her on the hall table, unlocked the door to find her belongings there but no sign of Melita. There was no sign of a disturbance and Melita's suitcases were still on top of the wardrobe. After some deliberation, she contacted the police.

Uncle Brad was questioned but explained he and his wife had been living separately for some time, and he'd had no recent contact with her. A full-scale search was set up. At this time in my life, I was barely old enough to read a newspaper, and in any case, ours seemed to be put smartly out of reach as soon as it hit the doormat, so most of what I learned hereafter was gleaned from over-heard conversations. For ages, there was no sign of Melita at all, and it began to look as if she'd simply run off with some man, as she'd done before. Then one of the kids from the Nissen huts in the park found a shoe.

The shoe in question was a red and black two-tone shoe with a platform sole, and her landlady confirmed that Melita had indeed owned a similar pair. The shoe had been found in the reeds by the edge of the lake, and a dragging operation began. They found Melita at the bottom of the lake in Priory Park, fully clothed and covered in mud. Except for her shoes. Then the whispering began. *Well, she'd been asking for it...That woman always was a tart... Only got what she deserved...* etc. There was no obvious sign of violence, although she'd been in the water for such a long time, it was hard to tell, but nothing indicated she'd been pushed or dumped there. Nor was there any suggestion that she'd taken her own life, though a rumour started that she might have been pregnant or seriously ill. It was probably a fabrication anyway. An inquest declared an open verdict. Imogen went to live with our grandmother, although even that was not far away enough to be impervious to gossip. And they never did find Melita's other shoe.

A year or so later, Imogen and Uncle Brad, who during all this time had never said a word against Melita, emigrated to Australia and I never saw them again. After a while, the letters and Christmas cards dropped off, and that was the last we heard from them. My father and Uncle Brad were always on good terms, but we weren't the archetypal close-knit family, and neither of them were the letter-writing kind. None the less, I longed to hear from Imogen. From the day of the incident in the ruined house to the day she left, we'd never spoken a word about what we'd seen. She was the closest I had to a sister, and I missed her. But that's the way of the world, I suppose.

A while after they left, I went back to Priory Park, partly, I suppose out of morbid curiosity. By this time, the land had been sold for development. Most of the trees had been cut down, and the park looked even bleaker than it did the day Imogen and I last went there. Much of the house was already gone, though it was a hefty Victorian pile – clearly hard to dispose of, but not of any great architectural merit. Even the remains of the Benedictine priory beneath it were not to be salvaged, since in those post-war years, with housing in short supply, nothing was sacred. Now the roof was gone and piles of rubble blocked the entrance to the main doorway and the place where Melita and her lover(s) had held their less-than-romantic trysts. Jagged remains of walls jutted up towards the sky, which was nearly as leaden as it had been on that earlier, ill-fated occasion. I pondered the words of the man who'd chased us away and threatened to kill us. Was it just an idle threat? Most of all, I thought about those last fatal words shouted after the fleeing woman – "And that goes for you, too!"

Imogen and I never told anyone. Imogen, I suppose, out of pride, and I because I would have hated to bring further disgrace and embarrassment to the family. I wandered down to the lake, soon to be drained, and kicked about round the reeds. The sky had gone a nasty putty colour again. Something caught my eye and my heart gave a great thud of fright. In the reeds was something red and black, half-covered in mud. I picked up a stick and poked until I reached it, but it was only a red and black sweet-wrapper, thick with slime. I dried my shoes on some grass and went home.

Priory Park is a housing estate now, remembered only by a small square of flower-beds and a children's play area called Priory Park Gardens, but apart from that, no-one would ever know a house with grounds and a lake had ever been there.

One day, when I was sixteen, I was walking through town when a girl in a shop doorway caught my eye. Not so much the girl, initially, who was about the same age as myself, but her beautiful wavy auburn hair just catching the sunlight. Surely, it couldn't be...

"Imogen!" I shouted. But she didn't respond. I walked towards her and called, "Imogen?"

The girl looked at me blankly.

"Sorry," I said, "I thought you were someone else. You're exactly like her."

"So?" said the girl. Her manner was defensive. "So what?"

"Sorry," I said again. Her voice sounded coarse, ill-spoken. Like her mother, Imogen had been well-spoken. "What's your name, then?"

The red-haired girl softened for a moment. "Melita," she said. "Melita Smith."

From across the Market Place, an older girl beckoned brusquely to her. She too had a mass of wavy auburn hair, though I couldn't see her face.

"What the hell's it got to do with you?" snapped the one I'd been talking to. "You want to mind your own bloody business!" and she ran across the street. Both girls jumped on the back of a passing bus and were gone.

I've often thought about Melita. Looked at old photos of her in some family album or other. It cannot be denied, Melita had a certain glamour. My mother once said that Melita was one of those people who looked glamorous from a distance, but had a bad skin which she tried to hide with a lot of make-up. I suppose we all have something to hide. Something we did or didn't do, a long time ago. My mother said Melita was one of those women who simply couldn't help herself. Did anyone know she had other children? Who was their father? And was it he or the man in the park who killed her? And were they, even, one and the same person? Probably not. Most probably, whoever did it was just one more in the queue. But I can never pass Priory Park Gardens without wondering.

Early Morning Rain

Every morning since we came here, I've been wakened by the sound of women's voices, laughing, singing, calling out to one another, the sounds echoing round the arched entrance of the local government building across the street. And every morning, I ask myself how anyone whose job involves getting up while it's still dark to scrub floors and clean cloakrooms could sound so cheerful. Or indeed, so beautiful. This morning, their voices ring like bells, for the air is damp and tingling with moisture. In the other bed, Dean is sleeping the sleep of the righteous, as he does every morning, while the dawn chorus of cleaning ladies and the rattling of buckets winkles in on my subconscious until I drag myself free of the covers and totter over to the window to look at the mountains.

It is still dark in the street, but above the rooftops, the pre-glow of dawn is just stirring in the sky. Soon the tips of the mountains will glow pink, then peach, then golden and finally ivory before blanching into the purest white of day as the sun hits the lingering snow, and I never fail to wonder that you can sit on the beach with bare arms and still see snow on the mountains. In fact, I never fail to wonder. Just wonder. That's all. Over the mountains lie Granada and the Alhambra, and the magical, tangled streets of Cordoba. All these things fill me with wonder, but to Dean they are just lumps of rock and places you pass through on the way to somewhere made of concrete, tacky shops, tower blocks and tourist traps, sizzling with potential money.

"Ah, possibilities there," he'd say, as we pass some crumbling *finca* that generations of families have sweated and toiled over for centuries before finally giving up or dying out. "Nice little earner," he'd say, every time we passed a café or bar with a sale sign. "Opportunity for development here," he would mutter, licking his lips, and this went on all day until he fell asleep and the busy little cash register in his brain finally stopped pinging.

It was in Cordoba that I saw the man with the guitar. He was sitting against the side of an ancient building in the Jewish quarter. Tourists wandered, guides bustled, cameras clicked and whirred, but the guitarist just kept on playing. Dean had vanished, as usual, into the office of the nearest estate agent and I got bored, so I drifted back to the street where the guitar player was sitting, his liquid music spilling out across the now empty courtyard and curling round ornate iron balconies hung with pots, geraniums and washing. He saw me, and paused for a moment. "Hello," I said. He nodded.

"Are you here for the tourists?" I asked.

He looked at me for a second in slight surprise, as if it was a singularly stupid question. Which it was.

"No, my lady," he said, with that simple dignity most Spaniards have, "I do it just for love."

And he carried on playing. Dean would never have understood that. I listened for a while, then walked away, though I took his picture when I thought he wasn't looking. And as I wandered slowly back towards Dean and the estate agents (too pricey, only for restaurateurs, footballers and total dick-heads, mutter mutter) and even though I knew it wasn't possible, the music followed me along the twisting street. Dean wouldn't have understood that, either.

I have a memory inside my head, or perhaps it's just a dream, of a white house, plain and modernist, like two beautiful white boxes, one on top of the other. It has corner windows, and the sun pours in through those windows in dazzling whiteness, lapping round the white interior walls, the wind rippling the crystal light like water, the swept, bleached floor reflecting the whitewashed ceiling. On a table in the middle of the room is a bowl of oranges. Dean cannot see this room. He cannot see this house. Dean can only see garish signs which say *English Pub*, *Fish n Chips* and, God forbid, *Bingo*. – "Ah yes, gap in the market here," he'll say, as we pass through some simple, unpolluted place, and the little cash register in his brain whirrs and pings faster than ever.

Dean did not see the eagles soaring over the mountains or the stooping herons in the jade green rushes by the Guadalquivir. Dean never noticed the lone woman on the bench outside the church in Malaga like Eleanor Rigby, the arched branches of bare trees caging her in shadow on the rough stone wall. Dean would never see the pinkish golden domes and spires of Salamanca, a city so beautiful it brings tears to the eyes just to think of it. There would be no gasp of wonder on seeing between the mountains the incredible walled city of Avila, its ramparts breaking the green slopes like a wave. This country, this country that tears my heart. This country that lies in the palm of my hand.

I slap on some makeup, a little haphazardly, as I can't turn on a light for fear of waking Dean. I start pushing neatly folded clothes into my rucksack along with my camera and bottle of water. It's my old rucksack, the one I had years ago, when I was still a student. Dean is always telling me to get rid of it. But the pushing becomes more desperate and items re-emerge and are thrown softly back into the empty drawer. He can keep them, with the suitcases and his half of our money. Dean is still sleeping the sleep of the righteous, and as I stand finishing my note, the sky outside is slowly becoming lighter. The note says:

> *I am leaving. Don't come after me. I hope you find what you're looking for. But I'm looking for something else. Sorry. Thanks for the fun times. I'm not sure where they went. Bye.*

I close the door silently and tiptoe down the stairs. The street is still quiet, apart from the distant whine of a moped, and the cleaning ladies have gone. Fine spring drizzle, so fine it tickles like cobwebs, drifts into my face. I cross the street and turn into a narrow lane that goes between the shops and houses. It leads towards the old road through the mountains. The sky is turning pearlescent now, and the day is unfurling with the softness of doves, as I turn my face towards the hills and walk away into the early morning rain.

Every Other Thursday

My name is Clarissa. It is a romantic name. I've never understood why my parents chose it, as they didn't seem to like each other in the slightest. Consequently, I did not grow up to be a romantic person. So while I wouldn't pretend that Mr Hoptroff was my one and only love, I suppose it's just possible I might have been his. One way or the other, he was certainly a guiding light. – But to begin at the beginning…

Way back in the Swinging Sixties, 1965, to be precise – and as a librarian I can be precise to a fine degree – I found students and spotty youths in general immensely trying. While my younger colleagues swanned around in pelmet skirts and Mary Quant invisible make-up, my own style veered towards the frugal and recycled. It was not only the students who were a source of grief, of course. More mature readers could be a pain in the arse, as well. Many's the hour I have spent researching the history of salt-glazed sanitary ware in the Trent Valley or the carpet moth in Derbyshire for absolutely no thanks at all. Resentment is an emotion well known to librarians. But I smiled politely as Miss Partington wittered on about the state of the nation while she dumped gruesome parcels of whitebait and liver on the counter and clawed about for her books. And I did not snigger as Mr Ormerod regaled me with the proven facts about the Lost Continent of Mu for there, I thought, but for the grace of God, go I.

Eccentrics apart, librarianship does have its boring moments. Wednesdays, half-day closing in town, were spent weeding the shelves, pruning the catalogue and filing "Keesing's Bleeding Archives", as one of the Pelmet-Skirts put it so poetically. Thursdays, however, were a different matter. Every other Thursday, a small group of inmates from Tamhurst Park Open Prison would bound up the stairs in their denims, like so many frisky Dobermans let off the leash. After giving the Pelmet-Skirts the eye, they would disappear among the shelves and riffle happily through the pages of *Rubens* and *Renoir* and *Teach Yourself Lock-Picking*. A fine cloud of cigarette-smoke would drift between the bookcases and Uncle Fred would drift after it uttering recriminatory words, but apart from a bit of nudging and shuffling, they were as good as gold.

"We get the cream of the prisoners here," Uncle Fred, the chattier of the two officers, would say. "Crème de la crème, our lads. Only book-cookers and bigamists at Tamhurst Park." Once the novelty of being at liberty among librarians wore off, however, they soon became subdued and downcast, perhaps afraid of being spotted by the wife's mother or somebody they'd conned out of an inheritance. Mr Hoptroff, the Prison Librarian, though, was a different matter.

Mr Hoptroff was dark and good-looking, with penetrating blue eyes and a most unprisonly tan. He was probably knocking on forty, but combined old-world sophistication with a boyish wide-eyed charm. Even the Pelmet-Skirts, despite a taste for younger stuff, couldn't keep their eyes off him. He was well-spoken and intelligent, with an interest in classical music. He had even, he confided, written a few bars himself from time to time. He assured me that his unusual surname was Russian, though as one of the Pelmet-Skirts remarked tartly, it was probably Anglo-Saxon and related to pigswill. One day, when our eyes met over a copy of *Chamber Music in the Eighteenth Century*, he gave me a prolonged blue-eyed gaze and told me how much my presence every other Thursday meant to him.

I had to admit, for me, too, Thursdays had taken on a new meaning. Hitherto, the only thing to look forward to was my weekly yoga lesson in a chilly church hall with a concrete floor. Resisting the urge to ask him if he'd care to join me later on my hassock – a pointless suggestion since he had to be locked back in his cell at 7.30pm – I bided my time and responded with an enigmatic smile.

The next Thursday I was rewarded with another gaze of burning sincerity, and the genteel comment that my ancient purple frock was a particularly alluring colour. This was accompanied by a smile so beguiling I had to open the nearest window. Had not Uncle Fred once confided in us that they used to put saltpetre in the tea to calm them down? As the aroma of damp coke from the boiler-room drifted in like fog, I thanked him politely and resolved to acquire another purple dress asap, perhaps with a lower neckline. And I wondered what it was, exactly, that he'd done to get himself incarcerated.

“You're most kind,” I murmured, inhaling deeply and starting to cough. He patted my back in a courteous manner and my bra hook shot undone with an embarrassing twang.

Two weeks later, as he was returning the book he'd borrowed on Schubert, he suggested I might find the note on page 253 particularly interesting. I did.

Clarissa, it began, *Clarissa – what a delightful and unusual name – Clarissa, I can keep this a secret no longer! We are soul mates – I love you...!* The notepaper was a trifle Spartan, but the sentiments made my heart sing. And again, I wondered – What *has* he done?

I enquired discreetly of Uncle Fred the following Thursday.

“Blackmail and extortion,” he replied promptly, adding as an afterthought, “and serial bigamy. The sentences to run concurrently.”

I knew some things were too good to be true. But even so, we did have a lot in common.

About this time, a new nutcase alighted on the library scene, a Mrs Ipstones, who dressed in gothic black and powdered her face with flour. Mrs Ipstones made a beeline for me for some reason, and was soon enthralling me with her passion for reptiles.

“I've got some lovely baby boa-constrictors in my bath,” she remarked one day, “You'll have to come round and see them sometime.”

I declined politely, preferring to spend my evenings mooning over notes from Mr Hoptroff and wondering whether or not to reply. At the moment, we relied simply on knowing smiles.

“I’ll bring you some pictures next time, then,” said Mrs Ipstones, accepting my excuse about lack of transport and ailing relatives.

“I'll look forward to that,” I said, praying she didn't change her day from Wednesday to Thursday. Luckily she didn't, so I was able to Coo and Ahh over the baby boas without sacrificing any precious moments with Mr Hoptroff.

Surprisingly, the boas did have a certain charm. I wondered if they were slimy. She assured me they were not, and blathered on regardless: “Oh no, dear, they're quite warm and dry. They enjoy a stroke and cuddle. It's quite sweet the way they snuggle up to you...” *– Ah, Mr.Hoptroff, give me half a chance.* – “I've got a monitor lizard and two Gila monsters coming by special delivery tomorrow. They're carnivorous, you know. I've had iguanas before, but never Gilas or monitors. I think I might treat myself to a marine iguana next, you know, the ones Darwin found on Galapagos. Hideous, but totally fascinating..." – *Oh Oliver Hoptroff, take me away from all this.* – "Just think what we might never have known if Darwin hadn't gone to Galapagos." – *Blackmail, extortion, serial bigamy? Well no, probably not...*

However, my romance with Mr Hoptroff or Oily Oliver, as the Pelmet-Skirts christened him, continued on its wary way. The notes in returned reading matter became ever more effusive and the gaze of Mr Hoptroff ever more persuasive. The messages had now progressed to *Marry me, Clarissa, let us make music together!* I had to sit back and consider matters. I was, after all, slightly over thirty, my career in the library had reached relative stalemate, and I didn't have any money. So what could an engaging ex-con-man and serial bigamist have to offer a girl like me? Well, dash all, frankly. Even if he *was* going to write a symphony and dedicate it to me. I would probably have to spend the rest of my life as a professional prison visitor and go down in history as *'Optroff's Eighth.*

Then suddenly, an event occurred which changed my life. Poor Mrs Ipstones succumbed to something nobody knew she had, and dropped dead. Perhaps no-one even noticed she was ill, since due to all that white yuk she plastered over her face she always looked to be at death's door anyway. I was quite sorry. But the truly amazing thing was, she left her house and all her earthly possessions to me. Mrs Ipstones had no known relatives, so suddenly I found myself the proud owner of a run-down Victorian villa and several hundred repulsive reptiles.

I debated whether to mention this to Mr Hoptroff, but decided against it. He was, after all, due for release in another six months. Nor did I mention it to my colleagues, since frankly it was none of their business and I'd never been one to socialise. So I continued to work at the library, flirt discreetly with Oliver every other Thursday, and occupy myself working out how to take best advantage of my good fortune.

The first thing I did was donate most of the rarer reptiles to the zoo and sell off the rest to Nastipets Ltd. However, I kept the python and the boa-constrictor, since I knew they were her particular favourites. Mrs Ipstones was right. They can be surprisingly affectionate. Once the house was cleaned and free from excessive croaking and slithering, I started planning what else to do with my unusual bequest. I thought about setting up a half-way house for ex-prisoners, then suddenly I thought, *Bugger that for a game. Time I thought about ME for a change.* And the snakes could probably do with a night out as well.

So I bought myself some new clothes with the proceeds from Nastipets and set about making good use of several years of yoga classes. Librarians are always above suspicion. Especially tall, slim, not bad-looking ones with a penchant for purple.

At night when I go out in my leopard-skin leotard or the lurex n' latex Rocky Horror outfit with bouffant wig, I'm completely unrecognisable. In homage to Mr Hoptroff, who inspired my new choice of career, I only do it every other Thursday. The rest of the week, I go to the library as usual, slipping a discreet calling card for the Uberlula Club (Exotic Dancer Night) into the right pockets as I tiptoe round the shelves. I *know* by the kind of books they read. The furtive glances, the sweaty paw-prints on the covers. I have my little list. The well-heeled warthogs who remind you they are Paying Your Salary when you charge them a teeny weeny fine. Lecherous lecturers, especially that porky music teacher who asks persistently for a work by Kodaly which he pronounces Hairy Anus, and once made me wait outside a concert hall in the sleet until the interval, for arriving two minutes late. Malevolent magistrates and crummy councillors. I give myself double points for anyone on the Library Committee. Every leer, every sneer, every unpaid fine, carefully noted. Ah yes, with unexpectedly furtive skill, I have snapped them all. And my only hesitation has been whether to offer the pictures to the Press or the Wife.

Now, as retirement looms, I'm more than happy with my life, and when I get home after a long day at the library, the python is always pleased to see me. The boa constrictor shuffled off its mortal coil some years ago, after an unfortunate episode with my accountant. They never found him. I buried the boa in the garden with a touching inscription and a mental note never to entertain clients (or accountants) at home. The art of blackmail and extortion, you see, is to retain an air of provocative aloofness. Never talk, and never allow intimacy. In all these years nobody's ever worked out where I stash the Hasselblad.

All in all, I'm more than content with my life, although perhaps it's time I called it a day with the Uberlula Club. The spare tyre, alas, comes to us all and with it, the realisation that a girl has to admit defeat. It's either that, or get a bigger python. I still get letters from Mr Hoptroff. They've seldom varied over the years. The envelopes still bear the logo HMP. Sadly, his periods of liberty have been few. Occasionally he still asks me to marry him. But I've always enjoyed playing hard to get. After all, the difference between me and Oliver Hoptroff is that he gets caught and I don't.

So when I finally retire from the library, I shall also hang up my purple peek-a-boo panties and python (metaphorically speaking, of course) for the very last time. I shall have few regrets as I sit by the fire curled up with a good book and the python purring contentedly in its tank. I shall take a hefty swig of Mrs Ipstone's fifty-year supply of sloe gin. And every other Thursday, I shall write a letter to Mr Hoptroff.

A Plain Brick House Surrounded by Fields

After leaving Mr Alperton's house, she sat in her car at the side of the road, trying to order her thoughts and fathom what or who she had just seen. Identifying the house from his letter had been no problem. But it seemed so far from anywhere.

The house was of plain brick, the ugly, dark red variety that looks as though it has just been rained on. There was no rain today, however, and the sky was a shimmering blue over the stark rectangular fields that stretched as far as the eye could see. The fields were planted with some dark-foliaged plants, potatoes or sugar beet perhaps, in perfectly aligned rows like knitting, or comb-marks through thinning hair. The soil between them was pale and sandy.

The house stood in the middle of all this, a little back from the road, as if deposited there by some giant passing bird. A straight path led up to the front door, with four neatly trimmed box trees, two on either side, like ball and stick trees in a child's drawing. The house, too, was like a drawing – absolutely regular, with a central door, a window either side, the same above, and one extra over the door. Edwardian, Victorian, Georgian – it was hard to tell, since everything here was sand-blasted by the wind, leached by rain and bleached by the sun. She imagined it in winter, under the wide, white Fenland sky, fields crinkled with frost, or icy rain slicing down, and always the wind rushing past like a high-speed train. (Do Not Step Beyond The Yellow Line.) Or maybe snow wrapping round it like a winding sheet or mist turning it into an island in a sea of nothing. And the inner voice in her head said, "No."

It was not this, however, that was disconcerting. It was the glimpse of the woman sitting immobile in the chair in the front room. Had she imagined that? There were coats hanging in the hallway, too, a woman's umbrella in the stand and what looked like a handbag on the shelf under the telephone.

"I thought you said Mrs Alperton was dead?" she said, hesitantly, so as not to cause offence.

"I did," he replied. Seeing her glance, he gave a little smile. "They can be removed," he said. "Call me sentimental. – Do come into the room."

She sat down in a hard-backed chair and looked around. It was a little old-fashioned, exceptionally clean and tidy, and completely silent. And like the hall, it smelled of polish and disinfectant and something else she couldn't quite identify. In fact, it was the cleanest house she'd ever seen.

"Can I get you something to drink? Quite warm today, isn't it?"

"A glass of water would do nicely."

He smiled again, showing perfectly regular, very small teeth, like a row of white seeds in a pod. His face was roundish and quite bland, with rimless glasses beneath a receding hairline, thin, finely combed hair, as perfectly aligned as those rows of beet.

"Of course."

He disappeared into the hallway and she heard him clip-clipping neatly along the passage in his polished shoes. A wedding photo on the mantelpiece showed him beside a big, sandy-haired woman, taller than himself, not fat, but firm-fleshed, with a large moon face. It wore just the faintest gleam of a smug smile. She looked about fifty and Mr Alperton looked much the same as he did now.

He returned with a glass of water.

"Thank you. I must say, the house looks wonderfully kept. It doesn't look as if you need a housekeeper at all!"

"All my own work." He smiled his neat, seed-pod smile.

"It must take up a lot of your time," she said.

"I keep a tidy ship. And so did Mrs Alperton." He paused to give her time to digest this information. "Well, Miss Fisher, I gather you haven't worked as a housekeeper before?"

"Not as such. I have worked in a hotel, as I said in my letter. And for a long time, I worked in a bank, until I was made redundant. I can provide references, if you like." She noticed her hands were leaving little sweat marks on her handbag. He wouldn't like that. She wiped them hastily on her sleeve.

"That won't be necessary." Another little seed-pod smile. "I gather you aren't married, although you did put 'Ms' on the letter. I never know how to pronounce that, I'm afraid."

"Divorced. Sadly, it didn't work out. – Were you married for a long time?"

He smiled again. "Only a couple of years. We'd both been married before, of course. We were very happy."

"I'm sorry."

"It was very sudden. I have to console myself with the thought she didn't suffer. Would you like to see the rest of the house, then we can talk about your duties?"

He led her upstairs. It was ordinary enough. Plain furniture, white walls made even brighter by the light streaming in through the windows. The beds neatly made – she noted two pillows on his – the carpets were immaculate, if a trifle thread-bare, the bathroom pristine. A faint whiff of toilet cleaner or disinfectant.

"I suppose this was a farmhouse, once?" she said, looking out of the back window across the great sweep of vegetable fields.

"I expect so," he replied. "I haven't really looked into the history. Most probably built for an estate manager. Or someone with a bit of money, the sort who play at farming but don't actually do it."

"You're not from a farming family yourself, then?"

"No, no. I had a dental practice in Spalding for many years." Another seed-pod smile.

Of course, she thought. The teeth. A flawless example of the dentist's art. Must have been a DIY job.

"I see." She ventured a hasty smile. – "I've always been a bit scared of dentists!"

"Oh, we're not so bad. Especially with modern drugs. Effortless Alperton, that's me."

He led her back towards the stairs. On a shelf below the banisters lay a huge Alsatian, quite comatose. The sight made her jump.

"Don't worry," he said. A tiny smirk. "It's dead. He was my first."

"First?"

"Mammal. Largest of my inanimate friends. Hadn't you noticed them?"

Weirdly, she hadn't. On the wide landing window ledge was a stuffed fox. It had perfect teeth, bared in a narrow grin. And in a glass case, a parrot. Strange, she thought, how too much light can be as disorientating as too little.

"It is an ex-parrot. It is no more." A tiny laugh, like pebbles rattling in a tin. A little joke to reassure the patient. Just inside the front door was a heron, tall and slender. She must have passed it on her way in. "It's my hobby."

"Taxidermy? Good heavens!"

"Not much call for it, these days, I'm afraid. Politically incorrect. But when I retired, I needed something to do. I could have joined a bowls club. Or taken up bird watching. Or collecting stamps. But no, I thought, do something different. You don't object, I trust?"

They reached the bottom of the stairs. There were more glass cases, containing heaven knows what, but he ushered her past them.

"No, of course not," she said, "but aren't they difficult to keep clean?"

"Not at all. A little light dusting now and then. The preservatives do the rest. Now, let me show you some more of the house."

The kitchen was spacious, light, airy, spotless. It needed some modernisation, but it was pleasant and practical. Several doors led off it.

"Pantry," he said, opening one briefly. "Only get those in older houses, nowadays." He whisked open others and closed them again. "...Broom cupboard. Linen store."

"That's what I like about older houses. Plenty of storage space."

"Absolutely. And I like plain, simple food, no problems there. You can cook, I trust? – Well, how do you like the place? Will it suit?" He had his back to the window, he was a silhouette. She thought he sounded anxious. "Will you take the job? It's yours, if you'd like it."

"I'm not sure," she said.

"No?"

"It's the remoteness. I mean, the house is lovely and I'm sure the work would be most acceptable, but it's so *far* from everywhere..."

"Yes," he said. "That has put some applicants off. Some of the ladies who wrote didn't drive, and that, of course, would be totally impractical. But you drive, and seem like a sensible young lady, if I may say so. I'm impressed."

"Well..."

"Will you think about it?"

"Well..."

"Well what?" He sounded a little irritated.

"Don't you ever get lonely here?" she hazarded.

"Not at all. Do you know what I like best about it out here? – It's clean. So clean. And quiet. The occasional tractor. A crow or two. Perhaps an owl at night. That's all you hear. Won't you consider?"

"I'll consider," she said, as he led her to the door. – "What about this other room? What's in here?" She indicated the room to the right of the front door.

"Oh, that was Mrs Alperton's domain. I don't use it now. She used to sit and read or sew in there. Or entertain a few friends from time to time."

Friends, she thought. Where from? Arkansas? The moon?

"I see," she said.

"I keep it much as she would have liked it."

He opened the door just a crack. A blind shaded the top half of the window, already covered by a net curtain. She saw upholstered furniture, a settee, an easy chair, and just for a second, she was certain, the top of a head resting against a chair with its back to her, just inside the door. A woman's head, with sandy hair. Then he closed the door again.

"Well, thank you," she said, as he showed her out. "I'll let you know what I decide as soon as possible."

"If you could make it within two weeks at the outside. Otherwise, I shall have to advertise again."

"I'll do that."

She sat in the car for a few minutes, then drove abruptly away.

A mile or so further on, she stopped. There was not another house in sight. She sat for a moment, then got out of the car. All around, the great Fenland sky arched from horizon to horizon. Only a slight rustle of wind stirred the potato fields. She stood there for a few minutes, taking in the vastness of it all. From somewhere far away, a cock crowed. She got back in the car. The woman. The woman in the front room. She *had* seen her. She knew she had. A big woman, whose head just showed above the back of the chair. A woman with sandy hair. She started the car again, reversed carefully to avoid the ditch, and turned back the way she had come.

The house was as silent as when she left it. This time, she parked the car a little further along the road on the nearside, where Mr Alperton hopefully would not notice it. Blossom on the apple tree at the far side of the garden was dropping now, but provided cover enough for her to slip in by the side gate. Keeping close to the wall, she glanced towards the other window by the front door, and could have sworn she saw the woman again, this time closer to the window, as if she were sitting there, looking out from behind the curtain net.

From the back, the house looked as symmetrical as it did from the front, apart from the number of doors. So, some of the doors in the kitchen were not cupboards after all, but opened onto the back garden. Storage for tools, or coal-sheds, perhaps. And the one to the left of the central door was ajar. Not what she'd have expected of Mr Alperton, who would surely have been cautious and careful in the extreme.

Pushing the door open softly, she stepped inside and found herself in what might once have been a dairy, whitewashed walls flooded with bright sunlight. Along the walls were shelves with bottles and jars, and several tall metal cupboards. In one corner was an old dentist's chair, complete with Anglepoise light and spit-bowl (once a dentist, always a dentist, presumably) and in the middle of the room, a large metal table. Neatly placed at one end of it was a surgical mask, a box of Dispensa-Gloves and a pair of handcuffs.

Handcuffs?

A door on the far side of the room opened very quietly. And there was Mr Alperton, in a pristine white lab-coat. Protruding from his top pocket was a syringe and a number of instruments whose purpose she preferred not to think about. He smiled his little seed-pod smile.

"I knew you'd be back," he said.

And with hideous finality, the heavy door closed behind her.

I'm Glad I've Seen You

She was on the bus again. That woman who thinks I'm somebody else. It was the third time she'd waylaid me. The first time, I was trying to cross the road. She hailed me like an old friend, "Oh I'm glad I've seen you! I haven't seen you for ages. How's your husband?"

"Well, dead, actually," I said, as apologetically as I could manage. I gave a brief account. I think he'd have seen the funny side of it. Although it *wasn't* funny, of course. And all the time, I was thinking, Who the hell *is* this, where do I know her *from*? Where've I seen this woman before? She went on a bit. The lights changed. The traffic moved on. All I wanted was to go home. Then she said,

"Yes, he often used to come in the shop, with his dog."

Er, dog... Yes, well, I really must be going. The lights changed again, thank God. I made my apologies and left, so to speak. Cat yes, dog no. Obvious case of mistaken identity. Later, I get a fit of the giggles.

"Then the man with the dog will come in the shop, she'll think he's supposed to be Brown Bread, then *she'll* peg out herself," said my daughter. However, some months or so later, I am sitting on the bus on my way to work, when a loud voice full of morbid enthusiasm hails me across the aisle.

"Ooh, I'm glad I've seen you! How are you?"

Confused, actually. Oh God, who *is* this woman? She looks pretty much the same as last time, though the hair-do seems different. The hair is sandy, running to pepper-and-salt, badly cut, though last time I thought it was permed. She wears a hairy tweed jacket in shades of red and tan, and this time a skirt. Last time I think it was trousers. She isn't smart, but she isn't tatty either. She's fairly non-descript, but then, presumably, so am I, or she wouldn't keep thinking I was someone else. She is a lot taller than me, however. And she carries an enormous off-white handbag with a huge metal buckle. Her accent is local. She could be anybody.

– A shop, a bar, a café… Yes, she mentioned a shop. But which shop? She goes on a bit. I'm not really listening and the bus is noisy.

I think somebody's got a hernia, but I can't tell who. She's sitting in the pushchair space opposite. *Why can't she sit in a proper seat? She hasn't got a pushchair.* Hopefully somebody who has will come along and make her move. I always sit on the side-facing seat behind the driver, because it's not quite big enough for two and I can usually have it to myself. I'm not as sociable as I look. The downside of sitting there is that I always end up giving a hand to anybody who *has* got a pushchair or has difficulty getting on or off. I'm not as callous as I look. And, of course, I'm a lot too conspicuous.

She goes on a bit more, and I nod and mouth "Yes" and "Oh dear" at intervals. Then somebody gets on with a double buggy (*oh, yee-ha*) and she has to move. She's penned in by the buggy and can't get over to my seat. There *is* a God. We lose eye-contact. I examine the houses, roadworks and construction sites passing by as if they were the canals of Venice or the palaces of St Petersburg (still Leningrad to me, sister, so watch your step) and try not to locate her.

"Well, t'ra then," she bawls as she gets off, shaking me out of my reverie. "And I hope you get on alright with your operation."

Thank you. Operation? Maybe it's me who's got the hernia, then. *Do* women get hernias? Or is that a pleasure purely reserved for the opposite sex? Medical isn't my thing. Maybe I'm thinking of prostate? Still, it makes up for childbirth. I nod politely, and other passengers regard me with interest. Then the door closes with her outside of it, and peace is resumed.

Next time, I am sitting further back on an ordinary two-person seat. Not a wise choice, alas. I take note this time of where she got on. She's still wearing the aggressively hairy tweed. She plumps down beside me like garrulous heifer.

"Ooh, I've been thinking about you!" – *Please God, no.* – "I haven't seen you for ages. How are you?"

"I'm fine," I say, mentally putting a ginger wig and dark glasses in my bag for the future use.

She rabbits on. "Of course, I've got the same problem as you…"

"Sorry?"

"With my husband, I mean…" – *Dead, is he?* – "Ooh, in't it awful, duck? Did he get aggressive towards the end?"

I feel like saying, "No, he was like that all the time", but I refrain. He did have his moments. I feel one of my own coming on right now.

"They say it always gets them like that, in the end."

"Pardon?" I am mystified.

"Dementia," she announces, rather formally,

Oh, I see.

"No, *my* husband had an accident. People were all rushing about during a bomb scare." She looks perplexed. "It was completely futile, really," I add, as if trying to make excuses.

She looks slightly aggrieved.

"Oh, I thought – " – The bus hits a bump, and the conversation veers off course somewhat – "Anyway, I can't get anyone to look after him. He ought to be *in* somewhere…"

I make sympathetic noises. Actually, she *is* a bit of a sad case.

"Doesn't know who I am most of the time..."

Well, that makes two of us. I wouldn't use the word pathetic, she's too assertive for that, but I *am* beginning to feel sorry for her. She goes off on another tangent, which finishes with, "And nobody *EVER* bloody listens to me!"

My stop, thank God.

"No," I say. "I'm sorry." I start to get up. – "I'm afraid I have to get off here." I notice, as she gets up for me, that the handbag she is holding has an initial on it. "J."

"Okay, well, bye then, Sasha."

Sasha? Good name for a model. Or a Siamese cat, perhaps. But it isn't mine.

"Bye, Judith," I say hopefully. – "Er, Joan…"

"Janice," she says sharply.

Janice.

It's late afternoon, some months later. I'm on my way home. As I reach the bus stop, I see there is one heck of a queue. I become aware of car-horns honking. I notice in my post-food-shopping stupor that there *is* a bus. It is full, and clearly it isn't going anywhere.

"What's going on?" I ask the person in front of me.

"Some idiot threatening to jump off the top of the car-park," says someone further down.

After a few moments, I decide to head for the nearest taxi rank. I am tired and my bags are heavy. It seems the only option. Traffic in the direction the bus has to turn is as solid as the Great Wall of China. However, if I shortcut back and across the market place, the taxi rank there will be free. I head that way, but as I do so, I glance in the other direction.

The car park straddles the road like a hideous six-storey monument to some unfortunate event. A crappy town planners' conference, very likely. In front of it, lines of jam-packed vehicles are in total gridlock. Horns honk and office-workers lean out of windows. Blue lights flash, and an ambulance is trying to edge its way cautiously between pavement, vehicles and gawping pedestrians. The car park straddles the road. The woman straddles the parapet. She already has one leg over the edge and looks like the other will follow any minute.

A voice from one of the gridlocked cars, male, irritated and thirty-something, suddenly shouts, "Oh, why don't you just bloody well jump?"

He's probably been there for a long time. Maybe he's just hungry, or wants a wee, or has kids to collect, but…

It does have the desired effect on the woman on the car park, though. Both legs are now over the parapet. A few jeers and tuts follow and the woman is looking very determined. She is sitting, right on the very edge. I notice she's still holding her handbag. Now what does she want a handbag for, if she's about to – ? – It's an enormous off-white thing, with a great big metal – *oh, bloody hell!*

"*JANICE!*" I bawl, "Get back off there this minute and don't be so bloody stupid. Get back off there *NOW!*"

There is a pause. She looks across towards me.

"Ooh hello," she calls. "I'm really glad I've seen you!"

She teeters slightly and the crowd gives an audible mass intake of breath. She looks down at them and seems quite impressed. "Ooh, look at all them!" she says. Then she leans backwards and is grabbed by two sturdy policewomen and disappears from view.

"So you know her, then?" says the officer back at the station afterwards. Janice has now been carted off in an ambulance to somewhere, hopefully, where they *will* bloody listen to her.

"Well, no," I say. "She only thinks I do. She thinks I'm somebody called Sasha."

I can see him squinting to check the witness statement I've just signed, to see if it tallies. I hope he might offer me a cup or tea or a ride home in a nice unmarked police car, but the days of Dixon of Dock Green are over.

"Sasha?" he says. He disguises a smirk. Clearly, I don't look like a Sasha.

"Yes," I say. "But I'm not her. Honestly."

He stifles another smirk and finishes off the form. Tired and still slightly shaken, it is very nearly dark by the time I get home.

Legal Aid

"We should never have come here," I said to Ben, as I opened the curtains cautiously. Prior to this, it had been impossible to tell whether the rattling sound from outside had been rain or dead leaves scurrying along the gutters. It was rain. The smell of brewing, flat and heavy, hung over the town like an ill-tossed pancake.

There was no post. *No change there, then.*

"Are you coming down?" I bawled, over the noise of the kettle.

"No."

"Do you want any tea?"

"No."

No pleasing some people. I put on my skirt and the brown silk blouse from Oxfam. It was smart enough, and made me look deceptively fragile. Ben was still a hump under the bedclothes. The rain outside had now reduced to a piddly drizzle. It was ten past nine. I put on my raincoat. It was signing on day.

"And don't forget to go to Telecom and ask about getting the phone put back on!" called the hump, as I opened the front door.

"What?"

"The phone!"

Ah yes, the phone. I hated confrontations.

"Can't *you* ring them?"

"It's been *cut off*, Asta, for God's sake!"

Ah yes, well. I'm not at my sparkling best till after 11am. I struggled to close the door. That was another of the things I needed to see the landlord about. The smell on the stairs was getting worse and more mouldy patches had appeared. The vacuum cleaner didn't work, the fridge dripped, and two rings on the cooker had clapped out. There were holes in the carpet and yesterday a large piece of the banister had dropped off. We had no tools to repair anything.

"Well, what do you expect for the rent I'm asking?" said the landlord, who lived twenty miles away and kept a post office in his spare time. He appeared once a month on Sundays to collect his rent and promptly vanished again. He was doing us down. In fact, that was all he was doing. I'd already decided to see a solicitor, and had spotted a suitable looking one with a Legal Aid sign in his window last week.

Ah, signing on day. I hadn't had any proper work for five months and Ben wasn't much better. Bar work was the best he could manage, and then only at the most unsocial hours imaginable. After which, he just tottered home and fell into bed like a damp glass-cloth.

I checked diffidently round the boards. There wasn't anything. There never was. I'd done all sorts from time to time, but I wasn't *that* skilled at anything. I could type, answer the phone, make the tea, all that sort of stuff, but people who wanted that wanted a school-leaver, not an out-of-work actress veering perilously close to thirty.

Maybe we should go back to London. More chance of work there. On the other hand, as Ben pointed out, we could end up sleeping in a cardboard box somewhere. At least it was central here, and quite pleasant once you got used to the smell. Or we could split up and try our luck separately. But we'd been together now for six years, and I didn't really see why we should.

The solicitor's office was on the corner of the market place, in the shadow of a church. The church was dedicated to St Modwen, who doesn't seem to have been heard of anywhere else, and was plain and delicate with sea-green windows. The solicitor's was a huddled red-brick structure jammed in between some Georgian townhouses, sheltered by trees that led down to the river, a small haven of tranquillity. The firm was called Dowle, Hoddle and Pepper, which brought a smile to my lips.

"Sorry, they're all at court," said the girl on reception, in that nasal automatic tone people use when they do this day after day and don't give a toss. "Except for Mr Dowle, and he's interviewing. I mean, you can come back in half an hour and see if he's finished."

"Can I wait here? I'd really like to see someone."

"Whatever."

Another girl was sitting in the corner under the window. She was well-dressed and gleamed slightly, as if she'd been sprayed over with varnish. She looked the other way.

I could see the tops of trees swaying through the window, giving occasional glimpses of the church tower. *...Bet St Modwen never sat in a solicitor's office waiting to sort out her landlord. I wonder who* *she was, anyway? Probably an early feminist, though... an abbess or something... Wonder who the patron saint of out-of-work actresses is? St Jude, probably...* A mobile rang. The girl opposite answered, covering her mouth with her spare hand.

"Yes, it's me..." *Who did you think it was, Abbott and Costello?* "No, open it!" *Open what? The vicarage garden fete? Joanna Southcott's box? Oh, a letter, what do you know?* "You mean I've got it?" *The plague, perhaps? Or possibly herpes? No such luck.* "Oh, I don't believe it!"

And with a smirk on her wet-gloss lipstick, she upped and went, without a backward glance. The receptionist, who was in a trance with an audio-whatnot clamped to her ear, paid no attention whatsoever. Half an hour or so passed. The receptionist unplugged her earpiece and stalked off. It was still raining, so I thought I'd stay another few minutes, just to make sure Mr Dowle, or was it Hoddle, or Pepper, hadn't died in the interim and might actually be able to do something for me.

A door opened and a head popped out and glanced towards reception. A slightly overweight body was attached to it.

"Ah. Gone."

I looked up and gave a tentative smile.

"Miss Jones?"

I gave a more positive smile.

"Do come in."

I followed him into an office, stepping daintily round waist-high piles of paper and cardboard boxes. Most of them were propped against radiators and some had collapsed into sagging heaps. A shirt on a wire hanger was hooked onto a filing cabinet. An unwashed tea-tray occupied a chair, together with an impressive collection of crumbs, and there was a pile of shoes under the desk. He knocked a few folders off a chair so I could sit down.

"Dead files," he said, with all the enthusiasm the subject demanded.

I smiled again. The fire department could have a field day in here.

"I've been looking at your CV..."

You what?

"Truth is, we need somebody in a bit of a hurry. Several candidates have turned down the job already, and..."

I'm not surprised. It occurred to me that I wasn't the Miss Jones he'd been expecting.

"Have you worked for a law firm before?"

Tricky one, this. Just then, the phone rang.

"Er… Not just now. I'm interviewing." He looked embarrassed. "Oh, alright, if you insist. Only, I have someone here… Erica, could you transfer this call to Mr Hoddle's office? I'll take it in there. – Sorry, Miss Jones, I'm afraid I'll have to leave you for a minute…"

After the door closed, I waited a respectable moment, then hastened to examine my CV. Or rather, Amanda Jane Jones' CV. She *hadn't* worked for a law firm before. In fact her achievements weren't all that impressive. I availed myself of the photocopier.

By the time Mr Dowle had returned, I knew pretty well all there was to know about Amanda Jane and had constructed a suitable persona to match. I wasn't awfully keen on answering to Amanda, but then I *am* an actress, for heaven's sake.

"Sorry to keep you," he said, sweating slightly through his expensive shirt. It had a turmeric stain across the tightest part. He wore a Rolex. "Difficult client."

Like hell it was. I know an aging Romeo fobbing off some woman when I see one. I smiled.

"Know much about legal matters, Miss Jones?"

"A little," I said, lying in my teeth. But then, my teeth are one of my better features. I gave him the benefit of a dazzling smile. "I'm sure I'll pick it up."

I'd been in a couple of Agatha Christies, after all, and starred briefly in a reconstruction on *Crimewatch.*

"I'm sure you will. We'll need your P60 and all the relevant gubbins. You can give them to Erica."

"To be honest," I said, "I seem to have mislaid those. My house was broken into a few weeks ago, and…"

"Oh, not to worry, someone will get it sorted for you. Let me give you a list of your duties. I mean, this will suit you, will it?" he handed me a paper.

I could do that standing on my head. We actresses are very adaptable. "Very well," I said.

"Right. Well. That's settled, then. Miss Jones. You are *Miss* Jones, I take it? I mean, you aren't married?"

This was true. Somehow, Ben never seemed to get round to it. "No, I'm still single. – How about you?" Cheeky I know, but I have charm. He cheered up slightly.

"Divorced. Perfectly amicable. Fiona sorted it for us. The best for both parties. Fiona's our Divorce Person. Super lady. You'll like Fiona."

I smiled again.

"Well, that's about it, then Amanda. – May I call you Amanda?"

"Actually," I said, "My friends call me Asta."

"Aster? Like the flower?"

"No, A-S-T-A. After the actress. Asta Nielson. She was a silent movie star."

"Gerald."

Poor Gerald was so terminally boring he didn't even ask me why I'd been named after a silent movie star, and a racy one at that. Well, it's a long story.

So the next day, Dowle, Hoddle and Pepper had a new legal assistant. It *was* less of a howl than a doddle, really. Pepper was seldom seen – just a smoke signal and a fit of coughing before he left for court. Hoddle was pleasant, busy, went everywhere at a brisk trot. Fiona, the Divorce Person, became a trusted friend.

And what of the terminally boring Gerald? Reader, I married him. And after that, I married Ben.

Men in White Suits

What were they doing there, the men in white suits? Every morning, looking out of the bus window on the way to work, I used to see them. Five of them: three close together, the other two further apart, close to the hedge on the far side of the field behind the houses. Five men in white Noddy suits, hoods over their heads, just standing there.

It was always at the same time of day that I saw them. Just after nine o'clock. Coming back later in the day, there was no-one there. Going out half an hour later, there was no-one there. But pass the field on the bus at five minutes past nine, and there they were. Somehow there, and yet not there. Men in white suits, glimpsed out of the corner of an eye, three together, two apart, just standing there.

One day when I wasn't at work, I walked along the road to see if I could get into the field. Sure enough, between the houses that stood next to the little wood, there was a gap, half covered by brambles. But there was no-one there. Nothing. Not a pale bush, not a bleached fence post, nothing that could create an illusion. And no men in white suits. Men who were there, and yet not there. It was just an empty field, rough grazing, though I never saw cattle there, with a narrow depression by the hedge, where a water trough must once have been.

I decided on a plan. If I left the house at ten minutes to nine, by five past nine I could be at the field. Then I might see how they came and went. But each time, something stopped me. The phone would ring, a bottle of milk would be there that required putting in the fridge. The postman would appear with a package for a neighbour. A procession of cars would cruise slowly along the road, so that by the time I got across, the deadline had passed. There was no-one there.

It occurred to me that I could ask someone in one of the adjacent houses if they knew what was going on, but I would have felt stupid to ask. I could find out who owned the land. I could phone the council. I could ask other passengers on the bus if they, too, wondered about the men in white suits. But of course, I didn't. It occurred to me that perhaps no-one else could see them.

I'd been feeling sick a lot. Headaches. Maybe it was the heat. It was very hot for early June. Then one day I was made redundant. *All this time you've been taking off*, they said. *Survival of the fittest, the company not doing well.* I got four weeks notice. I went to see my landlady. Her name was Mrs Rathbone. I'd only met her a couple of times, and didn't like her much. Usually I just slipped a cheque in the post. Strangely enough, she lived in one of the houses near the little wood. I hadn't been there before. The house looked slightly neglected. She opened the door cautiously, clearly suspicious. Then realising I was a tenant, she asked me in.

I explained the situation. Her mouth pursed. She informed me I'd have to pull my socks up, or I'd be out. No time for bad payers, she implied. No sympathy for lame ducks. I tried to explain I'd soon have another job. She didn't seem impressed. I wished she would open a window. It was very hot. Flies were buzzing against the window pane. Not far from the end of the garden was the field where the men usually stood. Of course, there was no-one there.

Mrs Rathbone's sense of décor was austere and slightly ominous. Not unlike Mrs Rathbone, in fact. There was this great big bronze Chinese Buddha thing on a shelf right above the door. One of those big fat ones that don't have a very friendly expression. Actually, it reminded me of her. Sort of malevolent and a bit toad-like. Perhaps that was why she bought it. Some inner demon made me think that if it fell off the shelf, it would completely flatten her. What an incredibly stupid place to put it. Serve her right if it did.

I picked up a newspaper off the settee and swatted at one of the flies with it. She opened the window. Thank God. She said she'd give me a few weeks to pick myself up. And no, she couldn't suspend payments or anything like that. She wasn't a charity. Then, as I opened the door to leave, there was this terrific gust of wind. I swear I had nothing to do with it, but the next thing, there was this God-almighty crash, and there she was on the floor. I swear it was nothing to do with me. And the Buddha lay there, by the back of her head. I stood it up again, and it just gave me the same malevolent, inscrutable look. Mrs Rathbone didn't give any kind of look at all, because she was dead.

Well, what would you have done? After I'd checked the pulse (there was none) I just sat there a while. Rather than actual injury, I think it might have been the shock that killed her. I shut the door and the window again. I bided my time. She was a widow. I don't think she had any family. No dogs, no cats, not even a cactus on a window ledge biting its nails. Probably no-one would come. I noticed a throw over the back of the settee. That would do nicely. There wasn't much blood. It was easy to clean up. I used a tea-towel. There's something to be said for hard floors, although I prefer a carpet myself. I sat and waited. Waited till it grew dark. I drew the curtains.

Then I rolled Mrs Rathbone up carefully in the throw and put the tea towel in with her. There was a ball of twine on top of the fridge so I made good use of it. It was like wrapping up a great big parcel, only much more difficult. Bodies flop about a lot. I suppose I ought to have felt sorry, but she wasn't a very nice person. Perhaps I should have said a prayer, but that would have been hypocritical since I'm not religious. Then I opened the patio door very quietly. Lucky the hedge had so many holes in it. I dragged my person-shaped parcel very slowly through the hedge and across the field. It took ages. I felt one of my headaches coming on.

The depression by the opposite hedge was just the right size. I covered her up with a load of weeds and broken branches, then I went back to the house. I wondered about the curtains. Should I open them again or leave them closed? If they weren't open in the morning, it might arouse suspicion. I decided on a compromise and opened them just a bit in the middle. Then I let myself out very quietly through the front door, locking it and putting the key through the letterbox. I'm quite meticulous about some things. As I walked away down the path, I found my headache had gone completely.

The next day, I went to work as usual. Actually, I'd be glad to get out of that place. They were a miserable bunch of gits, to tell the truth. I wouldn't miss them. As I passed the house, it looked perfectly normal. There were no figures in the field, either. Perhaps now Mrs Rathbone was dead, no-one would ask for the rent any more. It seemed a simpler solution than packing my stuff and leaving, which would also arouse suspicion. And anyway, where would I go?

There was nothing in the papers or on the news. Maybe nobody had missed her. Every day, the house looked the same. The curtains as I'd left them. No milk bottles on the step. I expect, being stingy, she got it from the supermarket, where it was cheaper. My headaches got better. I fannied around at work, doing next to nothing because nobody gave a toss anyway, and I'd soon be finished. I felt free.

My last day at work, I left the house with a spring in my step. The sun was shining. The birds were singing. The bus was on time. Then, as we passed Mrs Rathbone's house, I saw it. A red and white cordon round the house. Two police cars outside, and some sort of van, parked by the little wood. *Forensics,* said an informed voice, somewhere behind me. Everyone in the bus leaned over, gawping. And there they were, in the field behind the house. Men in white suits, three together, two further apart. Men in white suits, just standing there.

Cow

I look up the road, then down again. Apart from passing traffic, it is surprisingly quiet. Trees line the street – plane trees and limes showing a soft fuzz of new leaf, and on the far side of the pavement, laburnum, dripping with blossom, yellow against green. There is no-one on foot however, and I am lost. I hear the clacking of heels in the distance. I wait. A smart, older woman hoves into view, wearing several cows-worth of leather. I note, as she gets nearer, that she has a well-made-up, cross-looking face and creaks slightly as she walks. Possibly it's the leather. She looks like the worst possible person I could ask, but I have no choice.

"Excuse me," I begin, in my best trying-to-be-polite-but-assertive voice. She pauses very briefly, boot-heels scraping to a reluctant stop, face signalling the words, 'Don't bother me now, I'm superior.' She raises a haughty eyebrow.

"Sorry to trouble you," I begin again, stature already reduced, "but could you direct me to Lansdowne Road?"

She scowls. "You're on it."

I blink. Only a second ago, I'd passed a sign which said quite clearly Ulverston Street. Why do women like this make me feel like a provincial fifteen-year-old? I'm twenty six and nobody's fool.

"Oh, sorry, I thought this was Ulverston Street." Why am I apologising?

"Lansdowne Road," she snaps.

"You mean it changes its name, then?" Why, oh, why am I saying this?

"I think you'll find it's been Lansdowne Road for a *very* long time," she replies witheringly, and with a curl of her lip, continues on her way, faintly creaking. Maybe it's not the leather. Maybe she just needs oiling. I hope she breaks a leg.

"Arrogant bitch," I say to her retreating back, and from the sudden stiffening of shoulders, despite the leather, it's clear that she heard me.

Still seared by the encounter, I walk back to the street sign I passed. It does indeed say Ulverston Street. Ulverston. Where Stan

Laurel came from. The thought makes me smile. I'm not going to let a cow like that spoil my day. I prise the A to Z from my bag and squint at the relevant page in the bright sunlight. Yes, Ulverston Street *does* become Lansdowne Road, but is separated from it by a narrow unmarked lane about wide enough to accommodate a wheelie-bin. Perhaps it's called Oliver Hardy Alley, but the A to Z doesn't clarify. Checking to ensure The Cow doesn't turn round, I do a little dance to a silent *Cuckoo Waltz* and keep on walking. Today, after all, could be the best day of my life.

I am now running late, but nonetheless, I reach the bar in time. It is one of those imposing Victorian buildings with smoked glass windows, curly lamp-brackets and a discreet covering of ivy. The sort of place where straying aristocracy once picked up the better class ladies of the night, now popular with wealthy businessmen and their prospective clients. The drinks will be pricey and the food gourmet. I hesitate before entering. Will he be there? Will he mind the somewhat devious methods I have employed to get him here? And will he be pleased, after all, to see me?

"Juliet Sayle?"

And there he is. Tall. Distinguished. Eyes like wet slate under black brows. Even after all these years, I can understand what she saw in him.

"You recognised me?"

"But of course. – *What light through yonder window breaks? It is the east, and Juliet is the sun...*" He plays with the name like a well-bred puma patting something small and squeaky. – "Juliet!" The man's a walking cliché. Possibly reading my mind, he smiles.

"My mother had a strong sense of the romantic," I say hastily. My voice seems to be coming from far away.

His gaze combs me up and down. Still the ladies' man, then. The gaze sweeps round the room like the beam from a lighthouse, then back to me.

"And she was no doubt a beauty too, your mother?"

"I believe she was considered quite a looker in her day," I say, trying to make things rather less confrontational.

He smiles.

"In fact," – I'm blundering – "I think you may have known her."

I'm fishing. I'm putting out the bait. He's wondering whether to take it. Will he, won't he?

"Really?"

The guard is up. I've gone too far. Damn. Okay for him, not for me.

Then the frostiness dissolves. The steely eyes begin to twinkle. He's melting. I think he likes me.

"Well, it was a long time ago."

I think I'm shaking. I hope he hasn't noticed.

"I never forget a beautiful woman."

No, I'll bet you don't. Apart from one.

I smile. He smiles back.

"Well, about your work ... The Foundation..."

– I've chickened out. I'm back to being fifteen again. And gauche with it. –

I start again. – "I really admire what you do…"

"Yes?" – I thought the guard was back, but it isn't. He's interested. Definitely interested. The smile is knowing, but it isn't unkind.

I pause. A foot wrong here and I'm done for.

"Well…" I say.

The gaze combs up and down again.

"You know," he says, "it's odd, but you *do* remind me of someone."

"I suppose that's possible," I say. Do I tell him now? Do I take the bull by the horns? I hesitate again. He smiles. He definitely likes me.

"Actually," I say, and my voice now seems to be coming from further away than ever, "I have to come clean with you…"

"Yes?" Eyebrows arch. He's amused, but I think he's becoming a little impatient. He's a busy man, after all. And out there is money to be made.

"I haven't really come to talk about your work."

Eyebrows shoot up and down again. He must meet loads of little gold-diggers in his life. The searchlight gaze is back.

"So?"

I am naïve. I am foolish. I am gauche. But I'll chance it.

"I've really got you here under false pretences. I haven't come to see you about your work or the Foundation. I'm not here to interview you. I wanted to see you because…" – I'll have to take a running jump at it – "because I have very good reason to believe you may be my father."

A fraught pause. The eyebrows are doing the cakewalk. The slate-grey eyes blink.

"Oh my God!" he says. He recovers. The steely gaze sweeps up and down again. "Oh my God!"

A pause.

Then – "Was your mother by any chance called Ingrid?"

I nod, speechless. He smiles. Then starts to laugh. The warmth of that laugh washes over me like a wave.

"But this is wonderful!"

Yes, it *is* wonderful. It's incredible. It's amazing. He is pleased. He is touched. I've been waiting all my life for this moment.

Someone approaches. She is carrying a glass and is as yet out of focus.

"Heavens," he says. "I'm just so taken aback. Totally gobsmacked. But this is wonderful! – Juliet, my dear…"

She's resting her hand on his shoulder.

"Juliet, my dear," he says. "I'd like you to meet my wife, Miranda."

She's a smart older woman, wearing several cows-worth of leather.

Left Luggage

Tom Lane pulled his car onto the grass verge and opened both the doors. It was late spring and just beginning to get warm, though on this high upland ridge, nothing was ever warm for long until the summer was well into sway. On either side of the road, great swathes of grass and scrub stretched as far as the horizon, marked now by long whale-backed hills in every shade of green and grey. Less than ten years before, the horizon he'd seen day after day had consisted only of sea. Now, in this land-locked county, the waves were of grass, emerald green and olive, dotted with occasional sheep, the pitted remains of old lead diggings and circled ramparts that had once been a coral reef.

He took out his flask and lunch box and sat there, listening to the dizzy singing of larks in the clear sky. Tom was a commercial traveller. Not the sort that figured in bawdy jokes and comedians' stories – "I'm a traveller in ladies' underwear; I go for the black basque with scarlet trimming, myself, but I wear plain grey on Sundays," – which always made him smile, but Tom dealt in the more mundane matters of veterinary medicine. The latest in tick control, sheep dip and worming powders, among other enticing substances. Cows' udder cream was his raciest product. Many farmer's wives used it as face cream. It was a lot cheaper. He sometimes called himself 'The Last of the Medicine Men' – He thought he should be offering the wonders of Nebraskan Bear Grease or Kickapoo Snake Oil, with a by-line of conjuring tricks, juggling and a dance routine. Maybe he should adopt a headdress of feathers and a wampum belt, or wave a tomahawk about... He finished the rest of his cheese cob and tossed the remains to the chaffinches.

As he sat looking out towards the nearer hills with their crowning copse of trees, he heard an odd rattling sound along the road, and a strange figure paused for a moment on the brow of the slope to catch its breath. It was a woman, or at least, he was fairly sure it was a woman, since she seemed to be wearing some sort of tattered skirt and what looked like a cloak, with an old scarf tied round her head over a sun-scorched, weather-beaten face that was like a leather mask. It occurred to him that, if he was a medicine man of the Old West, then here was a squaw, a Cherokee or even an Apache – his knowledge of the tribes was a trifle shaky – or maybe, in these northern climes, a Valkyrie. She was astride an ancient bicycle, and attached to it were bundles of what seemed to be rags and assorted pots and pans, items of cutlery, and other ironmongery which was making the rattling sound. As he looked on, fascinated, she released her brake and swooped away down the slope, her cloak billowing behind her. She was like some human tornado on wheels, the bike's rattling and clattering accompanying her as she vanished into the dip then re-appeared on her own momentum half-way up the opposite hill.

He stood there for a moment, contemplating the strange apparition – a ghost, a spirit, a bird-woman, half-bird, half human, or perhaps just some travelling tinker? In these years not long after the War, a few tinkers still roamed the grey stone villages and towns, repairing pots and pans and whatever metal items had not been sent for war salvage, but they were always men. A gypsy, perhaps? She had the features for it, dark and hawk-faced, impassive, strong, a sort of beauty, almost... but then, he'd only glimpsed her for a second. He looked along the road again, but of course there was no sign of her. Now, she was far away, skimming the hills like a dust-devil, gone, out of sight.

He got back in the car and coasted down the hill, heading for the next town.

It was some weeks later that he saw the woman again. This time, near the stone circle. It was bigger than Stonehenge, but its stones lay flat and facing the sky. The weather was warmer now, but a small wind still ruffled the grass and whispered in the scant trees. From the track that led to the stones, he saw her emerge, silent and spirit-like, this time pushing the bike. He wanted to call out to her, but knew he should not. She reached the road, jumped onto the bike and was gone, swooping down the slope with her ragged cloak sailing behind her and, looking neither to the left nor to the right of her, she was up the next hill and away.

He looked after her for a few minutes, then walked down the lane and onto the track that led to the stone circle. The stones lay, flat and impassive, staring up at the wide, pale Peakland sky. The grass rippled like taffeta around the rim and dips of the circle, and he noticed that on one of the flat stones lay a small woven wreath of wild plants and grass. And he guessed instinctively who had put it there.

The farmers of the hills are a dour, taciturn lot, dark, long-armed, with their elongated moon faces, heavy-lidded eyes and high-bridged noses, so like the Basque farmers and fishermen he'd encountered many years before. He knew he would get little information out of them, but none-the-less, he wanted to ask…

"Have you ever seen the strange woman on the bike," he asked. "The one with the pots and pans?"

"Nope," replied the first farmer he asked. And the second. The farmers' wives were equally reticent. He tried a village shop, but the answer was still the same. Where did she live? What did she live on? It seemed like most of her earthly goods were attached to that creaking bike. Perhaps she didn't live anywhere at all.

Then one day, he drove into one of the small grey stone towns, hoping for an open cafe or a pub lunch, and there, parked by the little station, was the bike. He left the car at the side of the road, and wandered over. The bike was a work of art, folk art, really. Much more ornate than he'd noticed before. For it was decorated with bits of rag, ancient ribbons and strange cobwebs of coloured wool and thread. And hanging from the chassis, the famous pots and pans that gave it its distinctive sound as it rattled and creaked along the road. He stood looking at it in wonder. It really was a work of art. There was no sign of its owner, however.

Curious, he wandered onto the station and noticed that the door of the left luggage-cum-booking office was open. And there she was. On the counter in front of her was a large cabin trunk, and what he presumed to be its contents were spread across the counter. He watched as she added to the collection – a pair of candle-sticks, a glass bowl, pieces of china, a couple of pictures, some photos in a frame, silver cutlery, some items of table linen. There seemed to be no one else there, and she was entirely alone, oblivious to his presence. Each item was being unwrapped from pieces of cloth or tissue paper, and as she checked each one, she nodded her head, and put it on the counter. Then, after a while, when the trunk was empty, she began to pick up each item. Everything she looked at just once, then tenderly wrapped it again in its piece of cloth or tissue and put it back in the trunk like some kind of long-practiced ritual. Then she dropped the lid of the trunk with a heavy click and fastened a lock. At this sound, a man appeared from the back room and handed her a ticket. The woman nodded, took the ticket, and turned towards the door, Tom moving away to let her pass. No word was spoken. It was as though she had not even seen him. The man, meanwhile, had taken the trunk and was putting it away in a side room.

"Yes?" he enquired, as Tom hesitated in the doorway.

"I was wondering, what time is the next train to Chesterfield?" he asked, simply for something to say.

"You've missed it."

"Well, what about the one after that?"

"Four thirty eight."

"Thanks. I'll go and get some lunch, then." He paused. May as well ask. "The woman," he said, "the one with the trunk. Do you know who she is?"

"No," said the man. Then after a moment, he said, "We call her 'Twenty Three'."

"Twenty Three? Why?"

"It's the number on her left luggage ticket."

A pretty stupid question, obviously. Tom smiled. "Ah yes, of course," he said. "Obviously. Have you known her long?"

"I don't know her at all. I don't bother her and she don't bother me."

"Well, no. I just wondered about her, that's all. I've seen her sometimes, riding the hills, on that old bike. Is that all her stuff in that trunk?"

"Probably all her stuff. I mean all of it. Except what's on the bike." The man mellowed a little. "They reckon her husband left her years ago and she lost her home. Everything she's got is on the bike or in that trunk. She comes back every year, same time, takes it all out and puts it back. Then she goes away again."

"Where does she live, then?"

"Don't think she lives anywhere."

"Does she ever say anything?"

"No, never."

Tom looked out towards the street, but the woman and the bike had gone.

"Thanks," he said. Though for what, he didn't quite know.

The man gave a terse nod. He paused. "It's a funny old world, isn't it?"

"Yes," said Tom. "I suppose it is." And he went out in search of the pub.

For a long time, he didn't see her. He couldn't bring himself to think of her only as 'Twenty Three'. Yet the fact that she had no known name intrigued him further. Someone, somewhere must have known who she was. And yet, perhaps, it simply didn't matter. He stopped thinking of a name. For whoever, whatever she was, she was detached, aloof, beholden to no-one. She was free.

Sometimes, he fancied he saw her, sailing down the hills, a strange figure in black, like a bat or a swooping crow, or thought he did. Or was it just a shadow, a ghost, a figment of the imagination? How old was she, how long had she been riding those hills, silent, anonymous and alone? But did it matter? Did anything really matter? She was alone, she was adrift, she was free.

One day, he thought he'd go again to the stone circle. It was autumn now, and the hills seemed old and the rooks were cawing in the trees. He picked a few dry plants from the hedgerow, kecks, as his grandmother would have called them, and a spray of berries turning red as blood. He crushed some blackberries in his fingers, smelled their warm scent, ate one, then took a few plump ones in his hand. The grass smelled of age and sun, mushrooms and bruised herbs and all around, the sharp clean tang of limestone. As he approached the stones, he realised someone was there before him. There in the hedge was the bike, still with its webs of wool and rags, the pots and pans catching the low sun with a dull gleam. And on the biggest stone lay a bunch of wild flowers, cow parsley, vetch and a late, late rose. As he put his own tribute beside it, he saw her there, watching from the dip of the ridge, motionless, a silhouette against the sky. Then as she moved down past him, he smiled and for a second, saw pass over the weathered face a tiny softening, a drift of expression, the silent, fleeting ghost of a smile. Then she was pulling the bike from the hedge, jumping astride, and away down the long sweeping slope of the hill.

And although he rarely saw her again, he always watched for her as he travelled the empty roads, the Apache, the Valkyrie, the strange silent spirit of the hills.

The Hermit Crab

or

I'd Turn Back, Dorothy, if I Were You

Considering that all taxi drivers are supposed to know every street from Aardvark Avenue to Xenophobia Villas, only I could pick the one who doesn't. It says 'No Smoking' in the cab, but the fag hanging out of his mouth implies that either he doesn't give a toss or he's illiterate. I'd opt for both. We took one look at each other, and the animosity was mutual.

"Are you absolutely sure you don't know where this house is?" I ask yet again.

The drooping tail of ash drops off onto the seat beside him (I'd get fined £10 for doing that) before answering. "Never 'eard of it," he replies.

"And this is the end of the street?"

"Well, looks like it, dunnit?" A hint of sarcasm has crept into his voice.

"And this is definitely Eden Fields Road?"

"Well, it said so on the sign, dinnit?" (Not completely illiterate, apparently.) He sighs deeply and exhales nicotine fumes towards the roof. There is a pause. "Well, are you getting out, or aren't you?"

Something is familiar, yet the house isn't there. A feeling of foreboding hangs around, yet...

"Maybe I will," I say, feeling sheepish, but the thought of the long drive back into town with the Cary Grant of the Hackney carriage trade isn't exactly appealing, either. "Okay," I say.

I grudgingly hand over my money, making sure it's exactly right. I've had my eye on the meter for some time. "Sorry, got no change," I say snidely as I make my exit, being careful not to fall flat on my face. He grunts and does a three point turn a stuntman would have envied, showering me with grit. He misses the ditch, and, thank God, he's gone.

I stand there by the side of the road and survey the territory. The nearest dwellings are some distance away and don't look at all promising. Fields lie on either side of the road, and to the left, Eden Fields Road leads up hill and out of sight. To my right, a handful of shabby council houses, and behind them what might have been a builders' yard, derelict and disused. Some distance behind them, beyond the fields, is a small round hill with three twisted trees. On the other side of the road, invisible from here, is the river. I know where I am, and yet I do not know where I am. The fields, the builders' yard, the hill with twisted trees, are there. But the house, the house is not. There is no-one in sight and I am entirely alone.

The house, and I am certain of the name – is Edenfields or Edenfields House – Yet how do I know this? – and should be about two fields distant from the road on which I am standing, just to the right of the little hill. But the house – where *is* the house? Or *was* the house? The house was long and low, probably Georgian, and quite white and bright, standing out from the green fields. It seemed like the sort of house I'd always wanted. Every day for five years, I passed it on the school bus and looked for it. Sometimes it was there, and sometimes it wasn't.

The only drive from the main road leads to a red brick farm, not particularly old, and there's nothing in the fields at all behind the builders' yard. Was it to the left of the red farm, closer to Eden Fields Road? Memory plays strange tricks, and dreams play even stranger ones. I decide to head back to Eden Fields Road and look for a hidden drive.

It is warm and very dry, so walking is no problem. All in all, rude taxi drivers apart, it has been a very nice day so far, and I am on holiday, for goodness sake. I should be cheerful and relaxed. I am not, of course. I am as tense as a well-coiled spring, which is pointless, but that's the way I am. Probably I should try yoga. One corner of Eden Fields Road is sheltered by trees, the corner of a country park, once some wealthy person's estate, but the near corner, which is on a long, wide bend, is quite bare, showing sandy soil and rutted tracks beyond the scanty hedge. The pavement runs out here, so I hope nothing massive tries to pass me as I turn up the lane. However, I see and hear no traffic and the place is as empty as the Great Plains.

The lane is steeper and more winding than I thought and, after walking some distance uphill, my feet are hurting. Then, quite unexpectedly, a drive. Well, a track might describe it better, as it's overgrown and must be a sea of mud in winter. Thistles and dock and ragwort spring up on either side and, like the field at the bottom of the hill, it is deeply rutted with old wheel-tracks. I can see a broken pine on my left which I recall seeing from the main road. I must be approaching the little hill with the twisted trees but, because of the lie of the land, I can't see it at all. Folds and dips in the sloping hillside make it strangely deceptive.

Then, as the track curves round, I see it. There is the house, long and white and beautiful, looking out across the shallow valley. I pause, spellbound, then start to walk towards it. The house is still some distance away and as I get nearer, I see it is not as white or as clean as it looked. However, there it is, and much as I remembered. I am approaching from a slight angle, and as the track bends again, it disappears from view until a curve in the track leads towards the front of the house, but I see now something is wrong. From the side, I can see with a sudden shock that the back of the house no longer exists. The house is a shell, a whited sepulchre, only the front façade standing proud like a flat on a film set. Behind it just rubble, jagged remains of walls, bits of wire fencing and dilapidated structures that once might have been chicken coops.

As I stand there, taking in the destruction, I hear a voice. A man's voice.

"Hello, are you lost?"

He is standing beside a vintage sports car which must have come along the track behind me, though I did not hear its approach. He looks about thirty and has clearly dressed to match the car, in a brick-coloured sports jacket and corduroys. He has that clean-cut, sporty look you don't see around much any more. I gather my wits together.

"Sort of. I just wanted to look at the house."

He smiles. "Yes, quite a shock, isn't it." He pauses. "This is Edenfields."

"I remember it from when I was a child. Or at least, I thought I did. Only I've never been close to it before."

"I'm surprised you found it at all. It's a mess, isn't it? Sorry I can't ask you in for a cup of tea."

"Does it belong to you, then?"

"Used to. Strictly speaking, belonged to my old man. Long since dead, of course. I still come up here from time to time."

"I used to see it on my way to school. Well, sometimes. Sometimes I could see it and sometimes, I couldn't."

He smiles again. "Lie of the land, I expect. All came down in the Ice Age, boulder clay and gravels, dumped in heaps by a glacier. It slips from time to time, so you get little terraces under the grass. Then of course, in summer it's hidden by the trees. You must have seen it in the winter, when the trees were bare."

"Yes, probably," I say, glad of an explanation. "But I never realised it was a ruin."

"The house was badly fire-damaged in the Thirties. Family moved out. Then during the War, the Home Guard used it for target practice. Shouldn't have been allowed, of course, but times demanded, I suppose."

"What a shame," I say. He is looking out over the valley. Then he looks back at me. His gaze is peculiarly penetrating. I feel I should say more. "No, it shouldn't have been allowed," I say rather lamely.

"Ah, the folly of man." He has turned away from me, and I see him now only in silhouette. Then he turns back. "Would you like me to show you round?"

"Doesn't look like there's much left to show," I say, trying to lighten the mood. He turns back towards me.

"Oh, there is," he says. And he leads me round the front of the house. I can see now how beautiful it once was, although sparrows flit in and out of the empty windows and ragwort has sprung up in front of the main door. "Lovely, even now, isn't it?"

I can see how it was. I follow him around the far side of the house and realise we are now close to the small round hill with the twisted trees. There is a dip, then we walk up onto the hill itself. It seems so small, and yet when we reach the top, the view is astounding.

"And you thought there wasn't much to see, did you?" says my guide.

I gaze out across the valley in wonderment. On three sides, the landscape stretches out as far as the eye can see.

"Over there," he says, "is the Trent Valley – on a clear day you can see four or five of the power stations. Across that way is Nottingham, behind the hills. Over there is Loughborough, and those hills there are Charnwood Forest. Some of the oldest hills in the world – did you know that? 684 million years old, and if that doesn't give you a thrill, nothing ever will..." He is wrapt in his reverie. "And down there is Derby, hidden in a dip, can hardly see it from the air, you know. Never could. We always had problems spotting it, when I was flying." He turns again and points to the left. "Over there is the near end of The Chevin, and then the Peak District begins."

I smile in recognition.

"You know The Chevin, I suppose? If you passed this way on your way to school?"

"Yes, of course," I say. "We could see it from the school windows..."

"Imagine," he says, "what it was like under the Ice. Then before that, a shallow coral sea, then a semi-desert, then swampy forests, and before that, boiling volcanoes, spitting fire. Can you imagine the sea rushing up this little valley?"

I try, but it's all as mysterious and intangible as the house and the little hill itself. The panorama envelopes everything. Then, as we stand there looking across the massive vista, I become aware of a strange humming sound, like music. I can't tell where it is coming from, but suddenly it is all around us, vibrating and ringing like an orchestra tuning up, all on one note. We stand there, and the sound embraces us, travels through us, rendering us incapable of speaking or moving, entranced. Then, abruptly as it began, it stops.

"What on earth…?" I ask.

"Hummadruz," he says. "Nobody knows what causes it. I've heard it here many times. It may be something from the structure of the rocks beneath. Or underground water. No-one knows..."

He starts to move away down the dip slope of the hill and I follow.

I am silent. "I can see it's disconcerted you," he says. We are nearing the house again. From here, it still looks intact and inhabited.

"I never heard anything like that before," I say.

"Not many people have."

We reach the front of the house. It is a shell again.

He is moving towards his sports car, parked at the side of the house.

"I need to tell you something," I say, suddenly in the mood for confession.

"Do you?" I notice for the first time that his eyes are that strange slatey colour that is neither grey nor blue nor brown but something in between. He is really a very attractive man, but I am still disconcerted.

"I was haunted by this house, when I was a child," I say. "Then I forgot about it. Then, a few weeks ago, I had a dream."

He is still watching me, it seems, knowingly. I continue, beginning to feel foolish. "I saw a white house, this house, as I used to see it as a child. Standing alone in the fields, from the main road. It was like a film running in my head. And a voice said, 'Find this house and you will find something precious... Go to this house and you may find what you seek.' Or something like that."

He smiles at me, mildly amused. But it is not a friendly smile.

"You must think I'm mad," I say.

He has turned away from me, the sun behind him turning him into a silhouette again, a cardboard cut-out. "Sorry I can't give you a lift," he says, as he moves towards the car. "But your way and mine are not the same." It's as though the last piece of conversation has never been. "Of course, you don't live round these parts any more?"

"No," I say, disconcerted again. "I'm a businesswoman, built my own business from scratch. Fashion trade. I need to be where it's at. If you know what I mean. How about you?"

"Oh, bit of a chameleon, me. A hermit crab, more like," he says. "Move around a bit, fit myself into any available space."

"You don't look like a hermit crab," I say.

"Would you know one if you saw one?"

"No, but would you?" What is he getting at?

"Would anyone?"

He is still a cardboard cut-out, standing there with the sun behind him.

"Tell me something," I say, anxious now to change the subject. "Why did they leave just the façade of the house like that?"

"Perhaps as a memorial," he says. "Or a monument."

"A monument to what?"

"Perhaps..." he hesitates, "perhaps to the greed and folly of man," he says. "But I'll leave you to ponder over that one." Then he gets into the car. He faces me again, flesh and blood once more. "Sorry I can't offer you a lift," he says again. He starts the engine. It splutters a little. "Be careful of the lane, it's very narrow. They used to have tank trials up and down here during the War. That's why the bottom field is so churned up. You wouldn't believe it, would you?"

The car chugs over a few times, then quietens again. He leans towards me.

"I'll tell you something," he says. "I don't think you're mad at all. In fact, *I* had a dream the other night. I dreamed I went to a house, a plain suburban house, Edwardian villa. A red brick house with a bay window and a varnished wooden door. The door had a stained glass panel with an image of a swan, and each side of the door was a stained glass window with a pattern of tiger lilies. Along the path to the front door was a border of wallflowers. And a voice in my head said, 'Go to this house, and you will find what you seek.'"

He smiles, though the afternoon has turned cold.

"But that's *my* house," I say.

"Not any more," he answers. And the car moves away down the rutted drive.

Morning

Morning broke in silence, like something painted thinly on silver. A faint phosphorescence still glimmered from the as yet unseen sea. Every blade of grass glistened. But the two small figures making their way across this silent landscape were unaware of anything but each other.

It had been dark by the time they reached the church. Silent, too, save for the clicking teeth of sheep, nibbling at the tufted grass. As they picked their way carefully through the doorway around the fallen stones, the moon appeared suddenly from behind ragged clouds, illuminating the broken walls, as though welcoming them into that private space where men and women had once worshipped, now roofless and jagged, like a wrecked ship among the rolling fields. He looked up at the tower, round and corner-less, still protecting what was left from the savage winds that blew from the north and east. There was little wind tonight, though. Something to be grateful for.

"It'll do," he said. He spread the rug beneath the shelter of the tower. The rug smelled of horse, strangely comforting. "I'll miss the horses," he said.

"We shouldn't have taken the rug." It seemed like theft to her, though in the circumstances, perhaps it wasn't.

"There are plenty more. They won't miss it. They take better care of the horses than they do of us."

It still worried her.

"I never stole. Never in my life."

"Don't count it as stealing," he said. "Count it as a gift from the horses."

They lay there looking up at the stars. The clouds had passed.

"You know it was an accident?" he said. "You do believe me, don't you?"

"Of course I do."

"He was a bad lot. He deserved it. I only meant to teach him a lesson. I didn't mean to finish him off."

"I know," she said.

"Well, he won't bother you again. Or the other girls. Or beat the stable lads. Or anyone. Not ever again."

"No," she said. And she drew her cloak around her more tightly. "Do you think they'll find him?" she asked.

"They'll find him alright. It's when they find him. That's what matters."

He remembered the way the body had fallen onto the heap of mangolds in a corner of the barn. He'd covered the head with straw, not wanting to cause further disfigurement. In the dim light of the barn, the balding head and the mangolds looked horribly similar. Then he'd put more mangolds on top, carefully, so as not to spread the blood. It would be a shock for someone, but it couldn't be helped. There would be no mourners. Like he said, the man was a bad lot.

"They'll likely think he was out on the razzle," he said, "when they realise he's gone. Fallen dead drunk in a ditch, probably. They won't take it seriously till after a day or two, with luck."

"They'll miss me, though. But maybe not you, cos you don't sleep in the big house." Even in the dark, her eyes were still wide with fear.

"We'll have to take that chance," he said.

The moon had gone in again. It was very dark now.

"I'm cold," she said.

"Be glad it isn't winter. It'll be light early, anyhow. – You really can manage a boat, can you?"

"Of course," she answered. "My father was a fisherman. Same as yours. My brother's a fishermen. My grandfather was a fisherman. And my grandmother was a sturdy Dutchwoman."

"It won't be so bad with two of us, then. But what'll happen if the boat isn't there?"

"*Morning Star* is always there."

He pulled the blanket more tightly round them. "Go to sleep," he said.

As the first light streaked the sky, they made their way across the grass. Only the sheep were watching, raising their heads from their mechanical cropping and soon losing interest. Soft fingers of pink spread slowly, then dispersed. Then the pale sun. Shouldering their bundles, they moved quietly towards the village.

Stepping softly, she crept to her brother's door. She pushed the note beneath it, and they carried on their way. "Don't worry," she had whispered earlier, "They keep the Sabbath here..." And indeed, the village still slept in silence as they made their way down the narrow gully to the beach. The little stream that ran down it was full of tiny apples. Funny, she thought, that's exactly how it always was. They could be the very apples from their own cottage garden.

And there they were, the boats, just as she remembered. *Our Boys*, *Mary Jane*, *Eventide*, *Mizpah*, *Morning Star*.

The flints rang like breaking glass under their feet, but still no-one came. They finally pushed the boat free of the shingle, jumping quickly into it, tossing their bundles before them. The wake spread behind them like a silken fan as they glided out into the bay. He took the oars, not wanting to raise a sail until they were round the shingle spit that was barely high enough to count as a headland. As the village vanished from view, the first church bell began to ring.

"Do you think God really sees all that we do?" she said.

"Maybe," he answered. "But I don't think anyone truly knows the answer to that."

As the sail went up, the sun shone like a disc of silver through the fine haze, and the sea parted before them softly, with barely a ripple, the sky encompassing them in a giant shell of pearl. Sea and sky became one. But the two small figures in the boat were unaware of anything but each other.

The Armada's on its Way

Mam was a Spanish lady, big and bold, and wherever she went, we three kids and a sewing machine went with her. Dad was a Derbyshire miner, thin as a whippet, with a twinkly eye and a wit as dry as dustpan of clinker. He wasn't our real dad, of course. He died in Spain, long before we came to Britain.

Well, Mam was a proper Spaniard from Aragon, the driest and harshest place in Spain, and our real dad was a Basque miner from Vizcaya, hardworking, proud and political. When the uprising came in Asturias in 1934, there he was on the front line, wielding a banner. First time, they flung him into jail. Second time, they shot him. And that's all I know about my real father.

Now, the Aragonese are a proud lot too, maybe that's where the word "arrogant" comes from, and Mam wasn't one to sit around being the grieving widow, so she set herself up as village dressmaker, trouser repairer and general patcher-upper of clothes for those too tired or busy to do it themselves. She got hold of a second-hand sewing machine in a wooden case, cobbled on a set of old pram wheels, and trundled it round to wherever it was needed. Then she'd sit outside in the sun where the light was better, and rattle away on the sewing machine like a thing possessed.

Then the War came. Not the War you're all thinking about, the one before that. The one in Spain. And the Basque country, loyal to the Socialist Republic but staunchly Catholic, was right smack in the front line. The Nationalists, who were mainly fascists by the way, bombed the coastal towns, then they bombed the inland towns. Then they bombed Guernica. They destroyed the iron and steel-works, blockaded the ports and once they'd finished bombing us to bits, started starving us into submission. Apart from the lack of food and the fact that the house was falling down, Mam knew as soon as the fascists over-ran the Basque country, people like us – Marxists, socialists or revolutionaries of any kind – would be rounded up and shot in a ditch somewhere. So, she bundled what she could into an old trunk, rolled up our bedding and slung it on our backs and trundled off with three kids and a sewing machine towards the coast.

By the time we got to Bilbao, the quayside was teaming with refugees. The fascists were more concerned now with grabbing Madrid and Valencia than finishing off the Basques. So we waited on the quayside for a Welsh boat to come in. The Welsh were good to us Basques during the Civil War, and their merchant ships brought us food and took away families who had nowhere else to go.

To cut a long story short, Mam and my big sister Maria and my brother Roberto found ourselves in a tenement near the Cardiff docks, scraping a living from Mam's sewing until the day she met Dad. Dad was a miner, like our real dad, quite political, and he'd come down to Cardiff for a rally. He was a widower with four children of his own to bring up, or he'd have been off to Spain fighting for folks like us. Dad was a real character and the kindest man I've ever met. It makes me sad to think of kiddies today not knowing who their father is, and people saying step-parents are never the same, because our English dad was wonderful to us. Dad was very soft about kids, and he was lonely, too. Anyroad, he and Mam got married in the registry office and instead of four children to feed, he now had seven.

I'll always remember the day he first got us all together. We all crowded into the tiny parlour barely big enough to swing a cat, and Dad said, in his broad accent, impossible to imitate, but I'll try, "Right, this is your new Mam. Now, thee's mine and they's hers, but now you're all our'n, and I don't want any moaning or complaining or squabbling, 'cos now we're all one family, right? So we look out for each other, no fighting, no favouritism, alright? Now, you can all go out and play. Right, Mam?" Or words to that effect.

"Okay, boyo," said Mam. And that was that.

So we did. No moaning or complaining. No fighting or squabbling. Well, not much, anyway. Roberto became Bobby, Maria became May and I, Conchita, became Connie. And now we had Ivy, Betty, Jimmy and Sam as well. With so many of us crammed into a small terraced house, getting on was what we just had to do. And Mam and us kids became part of the community. Well, pit villages are pit villages, wherever they are and we'd only come – a long, painful way round – from one to another. Mam's warm heart and big laugh soon won them over. And her sewing skills were always welcome. If anyone could resurrect a dress or a shirt or a pair of work trousers from a tattered rag, Mam could. And her standard greeting of "Olá, duck," became known around the village. The men, however, tended to hold her slightly in awe, since Mam was, as Dad put it, a big lass, and carried herself with that special dignity most Spaniards have. Imposing, I think is the word. Tongue in cheek, they used to refer to her as The Señora. Dad had another name, though. She was a stickler for discipline, was Mam, and as soon as she came home from a shopping expedition or one of her women's meetings at the Institute, Dad would hasten to warn us kids, playing out late again, "Quick, inside, you kids – The Armada's on its way!"

And Mam would come steaming down the street, breathing fire.

Now, Mam and Dad were keen on one thing, and that was education. They hadn't had much themselves, and they didn't want us going out into the world ignorant. Dad loved music and opera and reading. Working class people then wanted to be educated. It wasn't that they were ashamed of what they were, but they wanted to better themselves. After the war, when the Labour government came in, Mam and Dad were overjoyed.

"Never be ashamed, paquita," Mam said once, "that your Dad was a miner – working class hero with heart big as football pitch, not saying your first dad wasn't hero too, bless his stupid Trotskyite heart. Never be ashamed to say you're Spanish because we are proud, brave and cultured people! Maybe you're English now, but Spanish too, remember."

Dad told us that even after losing their own war, 70,000 Spaniards fought for the Allies and about 20,000 died in German prison camps, not counting all those who died helping Allied airmen out of occupied Europe. And Mam said, "And see, look you, who was driving those first tanks into Occupied Paris. They were Spaniards, paquita. Never forget that."

Years later, I saw those old news photos and read what was written on those tanks, and realised what Mam said was true. There was Garbo, too, the double agent from Barcelona, The Spy Who Saved D-Day – but it was a long time after that I learned about him. And Mam's brother who died fighting with the Maquis. But the fascists still held power in Spain, and the sad story of the Spaniards who supported the Allies simply slipped between the floorboards of history.

Still, in September 1939, nobody knew what would happen next. Mam had gone through one war already, but like everyone else, she was resigned. By 1940, my eldest sisters, Ivy, Betty and May, were old enough to go out to work, and ended up on night shifts in a munitions factory. After five years hardly seeing daylight, poor May lost her olive Spanish complexion, but we all survived. Dad down the pit, Sam in the army, and Mam taking on an allotment, which she cultivated with great zeal. Her muscles became impressive. Her English had come on a lot, though still spattered with Spanish, Derbyshire dialect, fragments of Basque and a few choice bits of Welsh, but she got by. Me and Jimmy, the youngest, were still at school.

One day, while Mam was forking manure among her precious vegetables, she heard a plane coming closer. It was making a horrible noise. Then she saw some parachutes coming down. Not knowing whether it was one of Ours or one of Theirs, she kept a close eye on the descending aircrew, who came down in a nearby field. She could hear them shouting to one another, and whatever it was they were shouting in certainly wasn't English.

Wielding her fork, still viscous with manure courtesy of the milkman's horse, Mam headed on over. By this time, the airmen had disentangled themselves from their parachutes and scrambled to their feet looking disorientated.

"Hey you, boyos," said Mam, "Alemanos?"

"What?"

"Alemanos? You?"

"No!"

"Scotch-men, Irelandés, what?"

"Hey?"

"Well, what you, then?"

"Polski!"

"Ha!" Mam lowered her manure fork. "Español!"

Then she pointed to the parachutes and said "Gracias!"

By the time her brave Polish boyos had been ushered on their way with hugs and kisses, replenished with good Spanish soup, the parachute silk was safely stashed under the bed.

As 1945 rolled round and Jimmy was waiting for his call-up papers, Dad had an accident at the pit. He was laid up for weeks, and Mam nursed him devotedly.

"When this is all over, lass," he said, "I promise I'll give thee anything tha wants. – Within reason," he added hastily, in case Mam asked for a tiara or a holiday in Barcelona.

"What I really like, boyo," said Mam, dreamy-eyed, "Is great big all-white church wedding."

In view of the fact that Mam was an unabashed Bolshevik, who kept a small statue of the Virgin on the mantel-piece just in case, this was a trifle unexpected, but Dad took it like a man.

"Oh blimey o'reilly," he said. Dad was not a church-going man, and his family had been chapel rather than church, but he did his best. "Do I have to wear a penguin-suit, then?" he asked.

The vicar was duly summoned, and had only two problems – One, Mam and Dad were married already, and Two, Mam was very probably a Roman Catholic.

Mam drew herself up to her full height.

"Católico? No! Soy marxista!"

He took one look at Mam's biceps and agreed to do it anyway.

Naturally, Mam being Mam, she insisted on making bridesmaids' dresses for all us girls. There wasn't much around to make them with in the autumn of 1945, so we did what we always did – we made things do. And I have to say, thanks to Mam, we all looked fabulous. But she left her own dress till last, which perhaps was not a good idea.

"Off, off to the iglesia! Go!" she hissed through a mouthful of pins, as we dithered about waiting. We went.

And so it was, on a fine September day in 1945, Dad was already at the altar, and we girls and Sam and Jimmy and the vicar and everyone else were waiting with sweating palms as the organ kept on playing, finally, the church door creaked open. And there was Mam on Roberto's arm, with a mantilla of Nottingham lace and a spray of orange blossom attached to her big Spanish comb, majestic in many yards of parachute silk.

And Dad murmured out of the side of his mouth, ending with a great big smile, "Watch out all you kids, best behaviour now, The Armada's on its way!"

~ The End ~

More from Brenda Ray

Beyond the buildings, I can rise up now, above the cornfields, above the trees towards the blue mountains. A single shadow ripples over the stubble like a passing cloud. I have returned. I have come back. I am home.

These are the closing words of *The Siren of Salamanca and Other Stories* by Brenda Ray, and very comforting words they are too, to an armchair traveller such as me. Brenda Ray is an accomplished storyteller and seems just as much in love with England as I am. She is also in love with Spain but that isn't such an easy love. As she says in her introduction, *When I was a child, I dreamed about Spain. Not the place of cheap hotels and sunny holidays people think of now, for that place was only just coming into being, but a strange, wild place of wide vistas and blue mountains, dark cities and, very often, a sense of fear.*

As the attractive but deceptive cover of this book suggests, Ray's stories mix time and place, idea with vision, in a fascinating way, and if the cover tempts you to open the book, I don't think you will be disappointed. Savour the colours, the smells, the explorations of unexpected corners of the world, as I did from my garden chair in between bouts of English gardening, and overlay your experience of here and now with other times, other places; enjoy imagining the many ex-pats who have given in to the romance of Spain doing the same thing hundreds of miles away.

From an article by Kay Green 2008
www.booksy.co.uk